The Book of Lismore

An Archaeological Mystery

Yvonne Marjot

CROOKED CAT

Photography: Matt Gibson
Design: Soqoqo
Editor: Kelly Illingsworth

The Book of Lismore 978-1-910510-81-0

First Green Line Edition, Crooked Cat Publishing Ltd. 2015

Discover us online:
www.crookedcatpublishing.com

Join us on facebook:
www.facebook.com/crookedcatpublishing

*Tweet a photo of yourself holding
this book to @crookedcatbooks
and something nice will happen.*

This one's for you,
Ellie

Acknowledgements

Thank you to my fellow writers, both published and unpublished, for moral and practical support. One of the joys of modern social networking is being able to feel that you are part of a community of writers, many of whom are facing the same issues you are (and we all hate editing, believe me).

With special thanks to my writing colleagues Tracie Podger and Jami Gold, whose pertinent and much appreciated advice helped me wrestle with some difficult plot points.

To my daughter, Ellie; my sons, Daniel and Joseph; and my Dad, Mike, for your constant encouragement.

To Tabby, still my number one fan. Keep writing, lovely – I want a signed copy of your debut novel for my bookshelf.

To Kelly Illingworth, my lovely editor, for timely and helpful comments as we coaxed the story into shape.

To Laurence and Steph and all the Cats in the Crooked Cat cattery – the nicest publishing team in the world.

About the Author

Yvonne Marjot was born in England, grew up in New Zealand, and now lives on the Isle of Mull in western Scotland. She has a Masters in Botany from Victoria University of Wellington, and a keen interest in the interface between the natural and human worlds. She has always made up stories and poems, and once won a case of port in a poetry competition (New Zealand Listener, May 1996). In 2012 she won the Britwriters Award for poetry, and her first volume of poetry, The Knitted Curiosity Cabinet, was published by Indigo Dreams Publishing.

Her archaeological romances The Calgary Chessman and The Book of Lismore are published by Crooked Cat Publishing.

She has worked in schools, libraries and university labs, has been a pre-school crèche worker and a farm labourer, cleaned penthouse apartments and worked as amanuensis to an eminent Botanist. She currently has a day job (in the local school) and teenage children, and would continue to write even if no-one read her work, because it's the only thing that keeps her sane. In her spare time she climbs hills, looks for rare moths and promises herself to do more in the garden.

You can follow her work via the Facebook page and group, The Calgary Chessman, @Alayanabeth on Twitter, or on the Wordpress blog, The Knitted Curiosity Cabinet.

The Book of Lismore

"Dear Sir," he said, and the Salamander danced above the vellum, burning the characters into it, in elegant calligraphy.

Mercedes Lackey
From *The Fire Rose*, 1995

Prologue

I stood in front of the mirror, afraid to look. In the glass a tired woman stared at me, circles under her eyes, a haunted look on her face, one hand holding the neck of her dressing gown tightly closed. She was healthy and fit, with hair cut in a neat bob, and in other circumstances might have been considered attractive. It was far from the way I felt.

I summoned up my courage and released my grip, letting the dressing gown fall open. At the last moment I closed my eyes. I already knew what I would see.

A distinct line of bruises marked either side of my neck. Three of them on each side – the middle one was darkest, the uppermost sitting just under the curve of my jaw – and a pair of thumbprints, painted in shades of blue, green and yellow, either side of my throat in the soft skin above my collarbones.

I swallowed, still with difficulty. With my eyes closed it was easy to slip back into the memory: my back against the wall of my house, feet slipping in the gravel, hands grasping vainly at the fingers that were crushing my throat, his thumbs digging into my windpipe. I felt again his breath on my cheek and the rasping fury of his voice as he said my name.

He was so much taller than me that I had to stand on tiptoe as he hauled me upwards. In the end, my hands lost their strength and the light slowly faded. I felt it all go dark as I let go, knowing that the last thing I was ever going to see was his face.

A tear tracked slowly down one cheek, and I bent forward and leaned my forehead against the cool surface of the mirror, before turning aside to get on with my day. I opened my eyes as I moved away, and groped in a drawer for another high-necked jumper. There was no need to look at myself. It would be the same tomorrow, and for many days to come. But I was still alive.

1

Mud squished between my toes as I plodded up the track. I wished for a moment that I'd swapped my sandals for boots, but the mud was pleasantly cool and I shrugged my shoulders and trudged on. To my right crouched the two remaining Baliscate standing stones: small, grey sentinels standing guard over the secrets of millennia. The last time I'd been up this way was several years ago, when a university archaeological team were conducting a dig in the area. They put a note in the window of the Co-op, inviting any locals who were interested to come up and lend a hand, and I took them up on the offer on the third day of the dig, when the weather finally improved.

I'd failed to anticipate that, after two days of rain, the principal characteristic of the dig site would be mud. Rather than scratching delicately at the soil with a trowel under the watchful gaze of a real archaeologist, I spent two hours filling plastic tubs with water and disposing of it over the fence, as we struggled to drain the partially excavated test pits. At last the dig was declared dry enough and we all stopped for a brew, before sloshing out the last few container loads and getting down to business.

At last I was doing proper archaeology. They set me to work on a test pit in the middle of the site, between a fallen stone and a gap in the circle, where a missing stone might have been removed, or perhaps was still in situ, fallen and buried. Nothing came out of my pit bar a few flecks of charcoal in the soil, and after a full afternoon at work I decided I'd had enough. My shoulders and back ached, my fingers hurt, and my neck was so stiff I could hardly turn my head. I have no idea how archaeologists can dig for days on end. I suppose they get used to it.

The highlight of the afternoon came when one of the students spotted a bird of prey and asked me if I could tell whether it was a buzzard or a golden eagle. I told them I wasn't sure at that distance, but judging from the apparent size of the bird I was inclined to think it might be an eagle. The bird slowly climbed in lazy circles; it must have found a thermal, because it ended up as a dot in the heavens, joined by another tiny speck, and we watched them wheel around each other. I told the team that only eagles would climb quite so high, and they were over the moon with delight, promptly pulling out their mobile phones to text their friends with the news. I made my farewells and left them to it, but a few days later received an email from the expedition leader to tell me that soon after I left the dig site they found a cremation burial in the very pit where I'd been digging, complete with a tiny jet bead; all the more interesting because the nearest source of jet was far away, on the east coast of England.

Remembering my disappointment, I smiled inwardly as I passed the standing stones. At the time I thought I'd missed my one chance to find something really interesting. I couldn't possibly have imagined that a few years later I would literally put my hand on something that would change the established view of the history of Mull, and end up with my name in the local paper to boot.

By pure chance I found an object hidden in the sand dunes at Calgary Bay. It turned out to be a mediaeval walrus-ivory chess piece, probably similar in age to the famous Lewis Chessmen, and my attempts to learn more about it had led to the discovery of an unrecorded archaeological site. It had also coincidentally introduced me to one of the two men who were currently sharing my fantasy love life. All in all it had been a momentous year. I confidently expected this summer would be very quiet in comparison.

The path down the hill and across the marshy field was faint but easy enough to follow. I could see a little bridge that crossed the stream, and on the other side some helpful person had tied orange tape round the tree that marked the point where the path entered the forestry block. I had it in mind to climb to the ridge top and have a nose round the mediaeval monastic site, found by some local enthusiasts and recently investigated by Time Team. I'd been promising myself a visit ever since seeing the program. Who knows? I might surprise myself and find something the archaeologists had missed.

As I climbed slowly up the path, ducking to avoid the low, scratchy branches of some unhealthy looking pine trees, I began to notice scattered stones in the undergrowth. Some looked like natural boulders, others like fragments of fallen wall, and some even had scratches on them that led me to think about carvings and inscriptions. I fantasised about turning over one particularly large block, and finding a carved cross on its ventral surface.

Ahead of me the trees thinned, and I could see a patch of green and a glimpse of sky. I became conscious of the quietness of my surroundings. The pines shushed in the slight breeze, a sound redolent of peace. For a moment I thought I could hear voices, then realised I must be hearing distant bird calls.

No. It was definitely voices. There were at least two: a conversation, broken by sudden laughter. It was coming from the clearing ahead of me. As I emerged from the shade the warmth of the sun struck me and the voices suddenly stopped. For a moment there was only the sound of the pines, and then a figure stepped out from behind a tree on the far edge of the clearing. I started.

"Sam!"

"Hello, Mum."

"I thought you were on Lismore?"

"Um…I was. Now I'm here." I looked more closely at Sam. His shoulders were held a little too high and his face was flushed.

"What are you doing here, Sam?"

"Well, we were…um."

"Hello, Cas. Have you come to look at the site?" Niall

emerged from behind Sam and smiled at me. His welcoming grin was infectious and I instantly found myself smiling in return. Sam looked visibly relieved that the initiative had been taken from him, and wandered off to balance on a line of stones that definitely looked like a collapsed wall. I watched him go. My beautiful teenage boy had filled out over the last few months – his shoulders had broadened and he'd developed more muscle in his arms. As he teetered on a wobbly stone he reminded me of his toddler self, always ready to take risks and determined to succeed.

The tip of his tongue emerged from the corner of his mouth as he negotiated the tumbled rubble. A faint flush revealed that he knew I was watching him, but he turned his head away and avoided my gaze. I'm not sure exactly what a quizzical look is, but whatever it is I had one on my face. I turned back to the golden boy of archaeology.

"Hello, Niall. Long time no see." I can make small talk with the best of them. "Yes, I came to see if I could find the site. I wasn't expecting company."

"We've taken a rest day at the Lismore dig. Everyone needed a little time off, and I've been asked to have a look at this site, with a view to possibly producing a report for the local historical society. They're thinking about putting in a proper path with markers and information boards, so that visitors can find the site more easily, but before they do they need a full site report, in much greater breadth than the TV programme was able to give. I'm going to put in a quote for producing the report, although I'm sure mine won't be the only one. I had the RIB on stand-by and Sam said he'd like to keep me company. We're really only here for the afternoon. Would you like to join us as we look round the site?"

I'd seen the lifeboat crew's rigid inflatable boat in Tobermory harbour, skipping lightly between the moored yachts on its way to a shout. I had a sudden vision of Niall at the helm of his RIB, racing up the Sound of Mull with Sam crouched at his feet. Niall would be gripping the tiller, shading his eyes against the sun, the wind blowing in his hair – like a Nordic pin-up. It was a very pleasant image. I smiled at Niall and allowed him to guide me to the first point of interest.

Sam wandered back as Niall showed me round, pointing out piles of rocks that might represent house platforms, walls, the remains of a chapel. I sat down on a jumbled pile of stones, and Sam joined me as I gazed admiringly at one of the best looking men I've ever met, in his element, sharing his favourite subject with willing acolytes. He strode back and forth a few paces, flicking his honey-coloured hair behind his ears and waving his arms in the air as he pointed to interesting features.

Slowly a picture built up in my mind's eye: a small, quiet community going about its daily business. Beehive huts, or wattle-and-daub dwellings scattered about the top of the hill, centred on the chapel. Human voices mixed with the cries of goats, sheep or cattle, the distant voice of the stream, the quiet humming of bees. For some reason monastic sites always make me think of bees, humming their way around the herb patch and adding that little touch of sweetness to what must have been a hard life. Permanent residents may have been few, but there would always have been visitors: traders, curious locals, pilgrims coming to make offerings at the place of the saint.

Niall pointed out a ruined boundary wall hidden in the conifer plantation. "I'm going to recommend clearing the wood and exposing the layout of the whole site." He turned round again and looked at me. "You're sitting on the apse end of the chapel, by the way."

I struggled to see any pattern of buildings in the scattered debris. The most regular features of the site were some piles of logs where trees had been cut down to expand the clearing. Sam's foot slid on a wobbling stone and he leaned against me for a moment to get his balance, then straightened up and put his hands in his pockets, pretending it hadn't happened.

I looked at him sideways, while keeping half my attention on Niall's peroration. He was looking good. (Sam, that is. Niall always looks good. I wonder if he has found a girlfriend. I always thought he was wasting himself in his workaholic life, and here he is again, spending his day off looking at archaeology. On second thoughts, would any girl put up with it?) Sam had a slight tan and, bar a few scratches on his arms, his skin looked clear and healthy. At seventeen, he had sailed through adolescence with a minimum of spots and blemishes, and was turning into a very good looking young man.

"Any sign of white pebbles?" he asked.

Niall shook his head. "I doubt if there are any near the soil surface. Those would have been found in the initial dig. I don't want to disturb the site by digging into it – that wouldn't be appropriate – but I'm sure more will be found the next time the site is excavated. They were one of the key identifying features of the site, proving its religious connections straight away."

"How so?" I queried. I remembered the Time Team archaeologists shouting out 'another white pebble,' at frequent intervals, but I couldn't recall what was important about them.

"Pilgrims brought them. The stone symbolised the prayer they wished to make, given to the saint to ask him to intercede on the pilgrim's behalf. They might represent sins seeking forgiveness, illness seeking healing, loneliness seeking companionship; whatever need the pilgrim sought to fulfil would be placed at the feet of the saint and left in his care. The practice goes back long before Christianity – many a cairn in the high country grew out of the slow passage of people over the years, each adding a stone to the pile as they passed by."

"Sounds a bit pagan to me."

"That's a good point," said Niall. "I think this practice does go right back to old ideas about spirit of place, and sacred sites in the landscape. It's interesting that many Christian churches, all over Britain, have been built over, or near to, prehistoric ritual sites. Holy wells are an especially interesting phenomenon. They may well contain Christian era offerings, but could also conceal darker gifts from an earlier time. There's even a theory that churches dedicated to specific saints, particularly St Michael and St Andrew, map out the territory of one or two important Celtic gods. We may be able to learn a lot about pre-Christian peoples by looking at the development of religious sites."

"They didn't build this site on a religious spot, though," I said. "The standing stones are away over there." I gestured across the wooded valley in the direction of the sea. "Why didn't they build the chapel by the stones?"

"Perhaps there was local objection. Or maybe there was another site on this hill, over which the monks founded their community. We really have no way of knowing – but here's one interesting observation."

Niall beckoned and I scrambled to my feet, looking along the line of his pointing finger. He put his arm around my shoulder and pulled me a little to the left, so that my view was no longer obscured by a leggy larch tree a few feet in front of me. His grip was warm and he smelled slightly of sweat and a musky after-shave or deodorant. A wave of heat washed through me, from toes to head, and I fought down a blush while I concentrated on what he was saying.

"These trees were not here in the time of the monastic settlement. The monks had a view all the way to the sea, and the standing stones are directly in their line of sight."

He was right. I could see the standing stones atop their hill, well below the height on which I stood, and beyond them the track led onward to Tobermory town and then down to the sea.

"The monks were keeping an eye on that place. Every time they looked across the valley towards the sea they would have looked down on the stones, and no doubt prayed over them. They had the past firmly under their gaze. Besides, the stones are set in a very marshy paddock. Not ideal ground for settlement."

I stood still for a moment, trying to cast my imagination back twelve hundred years or so, erasing the distant houses and the noisy spectacle of a tractor, muck-spreading in the next field over from the standing stones. I could still feel the residual warmth of Niall's body against my side, and the grip of his fingers on my shoulder, but the man himself had moved. I turned and saw him standing with his back to me, side by side with Sam, the dark head and the golden bent over something Sam had seen.

I wandered over to see what they'd found. On the stones before them sat a very pretty dark brown butterfly, splodged with cream. It stayed for a moment, opening and closing its wings in a patch of sunlight filtered through the trees, then rose sharply and disappeared into the tree tops.

"Speckled Wood, do you think?" Niall asked.

"Yep," Sam nodded happily. "They live up in the canopy, but in the spring and early summer males come down to patrol territories at ground level." He nodded again in satisfaction. "Nice. First time I've seen one on Mull."

"There's another thing special about this site, then," said Niall. "It never hurts to present a broad spectrum of reasons to look after a place. I'll add them to the site profile, although Speckled Woods aren't a protected species as far as I know."

He turned to me and smiled that glorious smile again. (A little time away from Mr Webster and I forget how good looking he is. If only I were a few years younger. If only there was some sign that he's available.)

"How would you like to visit the site on Lismore, Cas?" he asked.

"Oh, I can't. I need to be on the last bus back to Dervaig, and I've already offered to cook for Hector while he's on his own this week."

"Sorry, I didn't mean today. We have to go ourselves quite soon, but I'll be back with the RIB in two weeks to meet with the members of the local archaeological society, and I could take you with me then. You can spend several days with us if you'd like."

"That sounds great. Two weeks' time I can definitely do, and I'd love to have a really good look at Lismore. I've never visited – it's not exactly easy to travel between

Lismore and Mull, without having at least one overnight in Oban, which is daft, considering how close it is."

"That's settled, then," said Niall. "Sam can phone you nearer the time and let you know the details."

He turned away and began gathering up his pack and various belongings. Sam took a quick sideways glance to make sure Niall wasn't watching, then stepped forward and gave me a brief hug.

"See you soon, Mum." With that they were gone, leaving me in a quiet, sunlit glade to contemplate the prettiness of butterflies (another hopeful Speckled Wood male had spiralled down to land near my feet) and the extraordinary good looks of the men in my life. I don't know whether to consider myself lucky or not – I've had damn-all affection from any of them – but they are very nice to look at. Look but don't touch. The eye of the beholder and all that. Is it more that beauty is only skin deep? My son breaks the rule, though: Sam is handsome and affectionate, and very good company too. I hope he finds someone really special to spend his life with.

2

Finding the Calgary Chess Queen last spring sparked off a flurry of activity. By summer it seemed as though events were happening almost daily, some raising fundamental issues that changed the way I would lead my life from that moment forward. Yet now, more than a year on from that grey, silent, lonely day, I feel as though I'm back living in slow time: long periods of nothing much at all, punctuated by brief moments of activity.

About the most exciting thing that happened in the last few weeks was waking up in the middle of the night to discover a late spring storm dumping a deluge of cold water onto my head. I ended up having to move my bed, turn out the mattress and all the bedding to dry, and pay a tradesman to carry out a quick emergency repair to the roof. Heaven knows when I'll be able to get the roof done properly, but that's what passes for excitement in my part of the world.

Sam, of course, dumped his amazing revelation on my head, turning all my plans and dreams for him upside down, and then disappeared back to school and his usual round of classes, prep, football matches and exams. He seems to have taken it in his stride and gone on with equanimity, as if nothing has changed. I suppose for him it hasn't. He already knew he was gay. The boy with whom he fulfilled that realisation has left school, and as far as I can tell, reading between the lines of emails and occasional phone calls, there is no one else.

Sam told me he didn't want another relationship, 'at least, not until I'm grown up.' I was completely in favour of that. In fact, the longer he stayed single the better. I shuddered to think of the bullying he might receive if he came out at boarding school. Besides, it was just one boy.

Just one life-changing experience. Maybe he wasn't really gay. He might be bisexual – he wouldn't really know until he left school and had the chance to meet a good cross-section of girls. There might still be a chance for me to have some grandchildren.

I mentally slapped myself. It's Sam's life, and his decision how he wants to live. I have no business parking my hopes and fears on his shoulders. Anyway, better celibate than promiscuous, regardless of whatever gender he finds attractive. One thing was certain, I reflected; he definitely hadn't told his Dad yet. Separation and divorce aside, I doubted Drew would pause for a minute once he heard Sam's news.

He would be straight on the phone to his solicitor, setting off a new round of vituperative letters accusing me of corrupting his son. Ironic when you consider it had been Drew who tricked Sam into going away with him on a luxury yacht last summer. A yacht packed with well-paid prostitutes, whose job it was to help Sam lose his virginity.

I'd been furious with Drew for behaving in such an irresponsible way, and unspeakably proud of Sam for keeping his head and managing the situation. Drew sees promiscuity (in males) as a sign of virility, although it would have been a terrible slur on his masculinity if he thought I'd had an affair. He probably imagines I'm still celibate. Having done my part of the job of raising his son (when permitted, in school holidays only) I'm now parked in an isolated corner of Scotland with no-one but myself for company. I felt a wry smile twist my lips.

To all intents and purposes I am celibate but, after a brief and delicious episode last year, reluctantly so. I've made my peace with Ewan, and the two of us can be quite companionable over a meal at his father's home, or on a run out with the dog. Ewan seems content with a return to our previous, mostly silent, encounters, enjoying one another's company without the need for conversation or physical interaction. I'm not.

The memory of our one evening of love-making still

inspires many a pleasant solo experience. My body woke up that day. It has never really gone back to sleep, and when I meet Ewan now I burn for him. It doesn't matter how many times I tell myself it wasn't meant to be, that it was merely the physical dance of two human animals – that it was a mistake. Still, I burn.

"Hey, up there."

I looked down. Bernie stood in my front garden. From my viewpoint at the top of the ladder she seemed to be extremely pregnant (again). Then I realised the bulge was the baby, strapped to her front in a carry pack. Beside her a small girl was picking daisies out of my unkempt flower beds.

"Hi, Bernie, I didn't hear you arrive."

"I noticed. You're standing on a ladder talking to yourself. Dr Bernie prescribes a break."

I turned back and looked into the gutter I was trying to clear. About half of it was still clotted with lumps of moss. I must have been talking to myself for quite a while – I'd got hardly anything done. I scraped out a lump of moss and dropped it on Bernie's head. It missed, but she shrieked and giggled, Tilly following suit as they danced out of the way and into my front porch. By the time I climbed down and wrestled the ladder back into its place behind the shed, Bernie had the kettle on and mugs ready. She pulled a plastic container out of her bag and gave Tilly something from it.

The child wandered off, eating, and bent to rummage through the books on the lowest shelf in my living room. She was a familiar visitor, and knew all about my wee stash of children's books from long ago. No one seems to remember *Noggin the Nog* these days, but everyone knows *Winnie the Pooh*, and my favourite edition of Robert Louis Stevenson's *A Child's Garden of Verses*, illustrated by Hilda Boswell, is a delight even to a child who can't read. Tilly dragged it out and settled on the floor, turning to her favourite pages. Bernie unpacked Emma and snugged her onto the sofa, between two cushions, while I settled into one of my battered armchairs.

"How's the roof?"

"Oh, you know. Leaking. I'm trying to clear out the gutters, in the hopes it will help, but I have a horrible suspicion the whole roof needs to be redone. More tiles came off last winter, and that must have made even more places where the rain can get in. In that really big storm I had to drag the mattress downstairs to escape the drips, and now I'm thinking I might have to clear out all the junk in the spare room down here and move into that instead."

Bernie regarded the pile of bedding in the corner of the living room. "You're like one of these ancient dowagers, living in one room of a crumbling mansion while the rest falls apart from lack of maintenance."

"Thanks," I said sourly. "Ancient dowager I can do without, though my mansion certainly is crumbling. It isn't only the roof; the guttering down the south side is all rusted, and half the water shoots out before it reaches the drain. The oven isn't working properly, the fridge is on its last legs and there's more rust on the wall cladding out the back, so it at least needs painting if not replacing."

My house was of an unusual style, even for Mull: tiled roof, but a timber frame clad in sheets of corrugated iron. Relatively cheap construction, but terribly cold in the winter. It had been the family's summer house before Drew ceded it to me in the divorce settlement. It was my sanctuary now, but it could certainly do with being a bit warmer, and weatherproof.

"Any sign of work?"

"Not a glimmer. Henry's doing his best, but he's had to lay off staff. He aims to retrench and sit tight, and if he does he should survive the recession, but there's no give left in his budget. He's doing some of the proof-reading himself. I know he feels bad about it, but he really couldn't afford to pay me anymore. I had that bit of housekeeping work last year, but when I fell off the ladder and hurt my back I had to stop doing it. I got a row from the woman – she was furious she had to find a new housekeeper at short notice and take on three changeovers herself – but by the time I was back on my feet she'd managed to find someone. There is work here, but you've got to be quick if you want it."

"Don't I know it," said Bernie comfortably. Jed supported her and the three little Kavanaghs on their smallholding, and he owned the equipment that was hired out, along with his labour, every year to other farmers to gather silage. The great, round bales of green grass, wrapped securely in reams of plastic by Jed's great machine, loomed in the corners of every field, slowly fermenting in the sun and rain, waiting to feed the livestock when fresh fodder ran out in the winter.

Jed had a third job, as back-up driver for Mull Explorers, a tourist company that runs Land Rover tours around the island. He was on call to drive one of their vehicles, if they were a driver short, since he knew a fair bit about the natural and human histories of Mull, and had a stock of well-worn stories he could trot out to add local colour. If all else failed, he could tell the (true) tale of Tom and the Runaway Tractor, a farming incident that still strikes cold into my heart. Tom's life had genuinely been at risk, but like all tales of daring and danger, once the reality was over it became a family favourite, and never failed to raise a gasp and a giggle from its hearers.

Bernie was quite keen to go back to work, but with two children still under school age and Jed working all hours on his various jobs, the difficulty for her was to find the time for it. My problem was a little different. When I left Drew, I already had shares in a number of his and his family's companies. I sold some to cover my move to Mull and to make the house habitable, and moved others around so that I wasn't wholly dependent on the Longmore success wagon. Though, despite our differences, I have to admit that Drew is a good businessman and his companies are sound.

Through all my difficulties in finding regular work, the dividends had paid barely enough to sustain me without dipping into my savings. The total amount of my capital was high enough to prevent me applying for unemployment benefits, but unfortunately since the credit crash my shares no longer paid out sufficient for me to live on. Some hadn't paid a dividend at all for two years running. As a consequence I was relatively capital rich, but cash poor, and I desperately needed any work I could lay my hands on to pay the bills and buy enough to eat.

There was no way I could spend money on the house, and even if I wanted to sell some of the shares, many of them were currently worth so little that I would struggle to re-roof the house even if I sold every last one. Essentially, I needed to knuckle down and survive for a few years until the market picked up and I could afford to fix the house. But the Scottish weather wasn't interested in my time scales – it wanted access to my house now, and was doing its best to arrange it.

Tilly squirmed into the chair beside me, dragging her book. "Read me," she demanded. I turned the pages slowly as she made herself comfortable. "Can I use your landline?" Bernie asked. She carries a mobile, but knew from long experience that she wouldn't get a signal in my house.

"Sure."

"Dat one," Tilly mumbled around the thumb she'd stuck into her mouth. She pointed to a picture of a girl leaning over the side of a wooden bridge, gazing into the limpid depths of a perfectly clear pool. I snuggled her into me and started to read *Looking Glass River*.

Tilly sighed contentedly as I got to the end. I squashed the end of her nose with my finger and she grinned up at me, the endearing, gap-toothed grin of a toddler without a care in the world. "How a child wishes to live down there," I repeated as she closed her eyes and the thumb-sucking noise grew louder. How I wished I was a fish at the bottom of a peaceful pool – with no more worries in my head than whether a fly would condescend to land on the surface and provide me with a free meal.

"All sorted," said Bernie, coming back into the room with a fresh round of tea and some toast. "Crap, I didn't want her to sleep yet. Oh, well, we can eat the toast."

"What's sorted?" I asked.

"Jed's coming round in about an hour to clear out your gutters. He'll have a look at the roof while he's up there and let you know how much you should be worrying. I've promised him a batch of your scones to take home – I can't be bothered cooking much at the moment, and my boys are constantly starving. I know how much he and Tom enjoy your baking."

"Thanks, Bernie. I'll make sure to tell him how much I appreciate it, but as for my baking – they wouldn't care whose it was. They'll hoover up anything edible."

"True," sighed Bernie. "It never ceases to amaze me how much they can eat. If I even looked at the kind of food they put away, I'd be the size of a hippopotamus."

I gazed fondly at Bernie, who was convinced she was fat, when in fact she was pleasantly rounded in all the right places. Unlike me. With my spare frame and small bones, I could pass for a boy if I strapped down the boobs and cut my hair. I don't understand why women with large breasts complain about them – they seem to be one of the top things on any man's list of desirable female characteristics. Not for the first time, I recalled Bernie's inevitable riposte: "You try running with two great weights hung round your neck: they give me backache, they get sweaty and sore underneath in the summer, and most men can't talk to your face – they end up fixated at chest level and talking to Pinky and Perky."

I suppose the truth is we're never satisfied with what we've got; there's always something to envy about another woman's body, something to dislike about your own. I really don't mind mine. I enjoy being able to throw on any old clothes and head out the door running whenever I feel like it. I find it easy to buy clothes – everything just seems to be in my size – and I quite like what I see when I look in the mirror. I only wish it was a bit more alluring to men. Well, to one or two men in particular.

Ewan was a dead loss in the attraction stakes. Whatever I still felt for him, it was obviously no longer reciprocated, and I still found it hard to comprehend, given his complete lack of response to me, how anything had happened between us in the first place. Something had gelled, between one breath and the next, and we had fallen into one another's arms and both given and received great pleasure. I didn't allow myself to doubt that. We had both experienced it. And yet, once it was over, it was completely over, as if it had never happened. Nothing in my limited experience had prepared me for that.

As for the other object of desire in my life, Niall Webster is as married to his job as always, and my childish crush on him seems to have no chance of reciprocation whatsoever. I tell myself I'm too old for him (a five or ten year age gap is nothing when the man is older, but it always seems different when the older party is a woman). Perhaps he has someone at home who is just not interested in archaeology and never goes on digs. That seems unlikely. I would say that the only way to spend any time at all with Niall would be to get involved in his work.

He doesn't even seem to be even aware of normal male-female relationships. His responses to me have veered from rudely abrupt to familiarly friendly – sometimes in the same conversation, depending on what he's thinking about – but I never feel he sees me as a physical being, even though I've been touched by him, casually and unselfconsciously, far more times than I've ever been touched by Ewan, the man who made love to me and showed me I wasn't dead yet. I wonder if I'll ever make sense of my relationships. Why is nothing straightforward?

3

I sat on a rock and looked at the sea. Behind me, Molly lay on the back seat of the car, snoring for Scotland. She'd just been on her longest walk for a week, and she was definitely showing her age. No more so than her owner – I'd left Hector at the hospital an hour ago, and now I needed to work out what I was going to do about Molly and how to let Ewan know that his Dad has pneumonia and won't be home when Ewan gets back from his fishing trip. I suppose I'll have to go back to the house and see if there's a phone book with Ewan's mobile number in it.

Failing that, it will depend on Hector improving to the point where he can have a rational conversation with me about it. Otherwise, Ewan will arrive home in two or three days to an empty house, sans father and dog. He'll guess pretty quickly that I probably know something about it, but will he be able to bring himself to contact me? Despite all my tales of self-confidence, I'm not convinced that he's 'over me' any more than I'm over him.

This morning started off being such an ordinary day. I did my little bit of housework (half a load of laundry and a few left-over dishes), looked over the garden and rejected it, and then sat down to try and write. In the absence of any paid work I was trying my luck at writing up the story of the Calgary Chess Queen. With difficulty. I enjoy the proof-reading for Henry, especially the non-fiction stuff, but writing isn't my strong point. I had the idea that if I could turn my real life drama into fiction I might be able to find a publisher. Would Henry help? Maybe, although I was reluctant to add to his burden of worries, as he'd deprived me of my only regular source of income and I knew he didn't really understand what a blow that had been.

I didn't want Henry to realise quite how dire my circumstances had become. Maybe I could earn enough to re-roof the house, and then work might come along. You never know in the islands – one minute there's no work to be had for love or money, and the next people are falling over themselves offering you jobs – but the writing was proving much more difficult than I'd expected.

By the time the morning mist had cleared and the sun had begun to burn through, I was sick to death of the sight of my blank screen. I pulled on my old running shoes and set off round the loch towards Hector and Ewan's place. It was a good time to run: still cool enough to stop me sweating overmuch, but late enough in the morning that a slight breeze had blown away most of the midges. After a couple of miles I ducked beneath some low branches and made my way round the back of Hector's house.

My route took me nowhere near Ewan's caravan, as I didn't want to risk bumping into him out in the open. I don't know why I'm still edging round the Ewan problem. I know I should square my shoulders, stride in there with confidence and leave him to have a problem with me if he wants to. It's just that I always feel he wishes I wasn't there. No sign of him today, anyway, and I made my way round to the front of the house and knocked on the door. There was no answer. Unusually, I didn't hear Molly barking either.

"Anybody home?" I called out, stupidly, as for heaven's sake they were home last night when I cooked Hector dinner and it wasn't as if he and Molly could exactly go anywhere on their own. That reminded me I didn't need to worry about Ewan. I knew perfectly well he wasn't home. He'd gone crewing on a fishing boat for a few days, which is why I cooked for Hector last night. My old friend is nearly eighty now. Although he keeps himself as well as possible, he can't walk any distance on his own, and relies almost completely on Ewan or me to walk the dog and run his errands.

Last night he hadn't been very well. We talked about whether his symptoms were a cold virus or the onset of summer hay fever, and Hector said he was planning to go to bed early and see if he could sleep it off. I hadn't been especially concerned about him – he just seemed a little under the weather. Now I was starting to worry that there was more to it.

I called again, and this time I heard a sound that raised the hairs on the back of my neck: Molly's voice, raised in a long howling whine. I'd never heard her make a sound like that before. "Molly?" I called, and she answered with a single bark. I cracked the door open and peeked in. No-one was in the hallway or living room, but Molly stuck her nose round the corner from the bathroom, then slipped back inside. I walked quickly to the corner and looked round. Hector was lying on the floor of the bathroom, moving weakly. I rushed to his side and crouched down.

"Hello, Hector, it's Cas. Can you hear me?"

"Aye, lass. Can you help me up?" Hector's voice was weak and faint.

"I don't want to move you yet. What happened? Did you fall?" (Stupid question, Cas.)

"N…no… I don't think so. I was going to bed. I felt very strange. My head hurts. I can't get my breath."

Sure enough, it had taken him several difficult breaths to get the sentences out. I felt round his head but couldn't find any injury, and Hector was struggling to get himself to his feet, so I helped him up before he wore himself out trying. Under Molly's intense scrutiny we managed to get to the old armchair in the living room, and Hector fell into it. I nipped into the kitchen and put the kettle on, then came back to see that Hector had closed his eyes. He was breathing shallowly and with difficulty.

"How do you feel?"

"I've been better," he said. He slowly focused on me. His eyes were bleary and bloodshot, and I didn't like the sound of his breathing at all.

"Hector, I'm going to call the doctor," I said, bracing myself for an argument. Hector prided himself on never going near the doctor's surgery, even when they phoned and nagged him for weeks about getting his autumn flu shot. "I never get sick," is his motto. "Why would I want to go to a place full of sick people?"

"All right," Hector replied wearily. I reached for the phone. Now I was really worried. The receptionist at the surgery agreed with my concern, but wasn't able to offer much help. "The ambulance is away down in Lochdon on a call, and the doctor is out on visits this morning. You've just missed the morning surgery. You can wait for the ambulance, but it could be quite a time. Do you think he's well enough to come in by car?"

I glanced over at Hector. He was looking grey and miserable. "I think I'd better bring him in as soon as I can," I said. "I can't tell how serious it is, but he looks terrible and he's having trouble breathing."

"Tell me all his symptoms," she said, "and I'll call the doctor while you're on your way. Drive carefully now, and we'll be ready for you."

Forty minutes later we drew up in the surgery car park in Tobermory. Hector was hunched over in the front seat, wrapped in a blanket and breathing in short, shallow puffs like a small steam engine. Molly sat bolt upright on the back seat, eyes fixed on her master's face. I reached round and gave her a pat. "You and me both, Moll." I opened the door to the surgery as Mairead, the surgery nurse, came out to meet us.

"Eochainn, a ghràidh," she said. "Ciamar a tha sibh?"

"Oh, glè mhath, a Mhairead," he replied, weakly.

She laughed. "Oh, yes, I can tell," she said, and led him gently into the nurses' station.

I helped her to settle him onto the bed, as she raised its back and propped him up with pillows so that he could breathe more comfortably. She began fussing round the bed, going through a series of procedures to assess Hector's condition, all the time chatting away quietly in Gaelic. As she settled the blood pressure cuff round his arm she patted him comfortingly and looked across at me. Her eyes gleamed and she smiled as she asked, "Do you have the

Gaelic, a charaidh?"

"No," I said. "I keep meaning to go to classes, but you know how it is."

"Ah, well," she said, and noted the blood pressure reading in her chart.

"What did you and Hector say to each other when we were coming in?" I asked.

"I asked Hector how he was feeling and he said he was very well."

I laughed and she grinned at me conspiratorially. "Men," she said.

Hector grunted and looked sheepish, and then we all laughed.

"That's a more cheerful sound than I expected." Doctor Allinson was in the doorway, and strode straight across to Hector to take his pulse. Mairead held up the chart and he looked it over. "Let's have a listen to that chest, shall we?"

I wandered into the corridor to give Hector some privacy, and then out to the car park to check on Molly. I rummaged round in the boot and found Sam's old Frisbee – heaven knows how long it had been there. It had enough curvature to hold a little bit of water, and I filled it at the outside tap and offered it to Molly. She lapped at it, but clearly wasn't thirsty. That's not surprising – if she sat in the bathroom all night with Hector she could have easily drunk from the toilet, and thinking of some of the things she'd eaten or rolled in while we were out for walks, it wouldn't surprise me at all if she had. We kept each other company for quite a while, and then Mairead stuck her head out of the surgery door and called me in.

"Mr MacInnes has pneumonia," said Dr Allinson. "I'd like to admit him to hospital for a few days, so we can keep an eye on him. I've given him something for the pain, and they'll get him started on antibiotics. Fortunately we're on to it quickly and he's not dehydrated yet, although I'll be happier once we've got him comfortable and he can have a cup of tea."

"Uisge," muttered Hector grumpily as we talked over his

head.

"No whisky," said Dr Allinson, firmly. "Plenty of fluids and we'll soon have you back on your feet." He looked at me. "Are you family?"

"No, I'm just a friend. His son's away fishing at the moment. I might not be able to contact him for a few days. I'll try and let him know as soon as I can, though."

I ran Hector down to Craignure in the car and checked him into the island's hospital. The staff nurse was expecting him, and was ready to set up a drip and start feeding in the antibiotics. I reassured Hector that I'd look after Molly and left them to it; and that brought me full circle. I sat on a rock at the side of Loch na Keal, staring out to sea and wondering what to do now.

Actually, there wasn't much to wonder about. I needed to go back to Hector's and check that everything was turned off and secure, pick up a few things he might need in hospital, look for Ewan's phone number and contact him if possible, take Molly home with me for a few days and otherwise carry on with my usual routine. Perhaps it was just as well I didn't have a job.

Not yet, though. At the moment I didn't want to move a muscle. The warmth bearing down on my shoulders was wonderful, and I felt sleepy and contented. It was one of those hot, summer afternoons without a breath of wind. The sun struck hard on the brassy surface of the sea, and its reflections were too bright to look at.

Out at the edge of the light-show a seal lay, presumably on a rock that was barely submerged. It was doing that magical thing common seals do – curved up fore and hind in a banana-shape, impossibly balanced on the surface of the ocean. It wasn't as convincing an illusion as some I've seen, since today the golden reflections of the sun made the water look like a solid brass platter.

A few feet in front of me, tiny ripples struck the shore making hardly a sound. The water was so clear at the shoreline that I could see pebbles and waving seaweed several feet below the surface. Suddenly, with a whoosh, an otter surfaced, poking its head up directly in front of me. I froze and it turned over on its back, holding something in its paws as it floated at the surface. I thought at first it was a stone, but when I saw movement I realised it was a crab. The otter casually gnawed off one of the crab's claws and lay crunching it, bobbing slightly in the tiny swells.

After a few moments it started, and looked directly at me. I was certain I hadn't moved, but perhaps I'd blinked too quickly, or a slight shift of breeze had brought the otter my scent. It gazed at me for a few seconds, then calmly turned over and disappeared under the surface. I glimpsed its body briefly as it moved into the seaweed and then it was gone.

I let out a gasp and allowed myself to breathe again. When I looked out to sea again the seal had gone, but the great, brazen plate of the ocean rolled on out to the horizon and the whole landscape was completely peaceful.

4

Saturday. A busy end to a busy week. I got through two changeovers this morning, after a late night call on Friday from a desperate holiday-home owner whose usual helper had broken her leg in a quad bike accident. Not someone I'd worked for before – it was nice to know the grapevine was working in my favour. The houses weren't particularly dirty, although in the second one a frazzled family weren't quite ready to leave when I turned up at twelve o'clock ('departure time 10:30 a.m. Please be prompt').

I worked around them, doing the bedrooms while they got their kids and luggage piled into their car and shot off, running a bit late for the early afternoon ferry. I hoped they made it. As usual, road works are underway on the island's main route and delays of up to forty minutes are the order of the day. It didn't take me long to finish off the house once it was empty, and then I took Molly for a quick walk before sharing my sandwiches and a bottle of warm water with her.

Mid-afternoon I finally took a call from Ewan and was able to drop Molly off at home. Ewan had called in to the hospital on his way home from the ferry, and reported that Hector was looking better. I happily dumped Molly on him and left him to deal with things. I'd seen Hector yesterday, so I knew he was on the mend. He was very annoyed with the staff when they wouldn't allow him to go outside and talk to Molly. I was quite sure that desire to see her, and to get back to the comfort and security of his own home, would push his convalescence on as quickly as all the medical care he was receiving.

Now I had to grab my bags and head off to Tobermory on the afternoon bus, in time to meet Niall and Sam after their meeting with the local historical society. I felt a bit guilty that I hadn't joined the society, even though finding the chess queen had given me a taste for Mull's past. I've never been much of a joiner. The meeting was due to wind up at about 4 p.m. and I knew Niall and Sam wanted a quick getaway, to pick up some shopping and get us all back to Lismore in time to feed his workers.

As it was I caught the bus with time to spare, and ended up waiting for them at the pontoons. They jogged up a few minutes later, laden with bags from the Co-op and the local Chinese takeaway. Feeding the workers indeed. In no time at all we were swinging away from the pontoons, out past Calve Island and into the Sound of Mull.

The air was cool and I could smell the salt spray leaping up from either side of the bow as Niall brought us round in a sweeping curve towards the south. I looked back for a few moments. I would have said I'd never seen Tobermory from the sea before, but realised immediately that the view was familiar from umpteen postcards and posters, and even a recent TV advert which showed the seaplane swooping in over the bay.

I'm never entirely sure how I feel about Tobermory. The town is pretty enough, especially the famous coloured houses set around the rim of the harbour. It's too small to have a complete array of useful shops, but feels too big and busy to fit my ideal vision of a Hebridean town. It's a nice place to visit, and I have friends there, but I'm always happy to get home. Somehow that nine mile drive over the switchback road to Dervaig slows you down, and bend by hairpin bend takes you into another place – a place that had welcomed me and become my home.

My neck was getting stiff in the brisk wind and I turned to face forward. Niall had wasted no time getting us well down the Sound and it seemed only a few minutes later that Lismore came into sight. We slowed and pulled in towards shore to give the ferry plenty of space to pass by the lighthouse. Niall waited until the ferry's wake had subsided, and then swung the boat carefully through the tide race and left into the Lynn of Lorn. The dig site was in a sheltered bay halfway up the south-eastern flank of Lismore. We turned shoreward and immediately the slight swell subsided as we came into the lee of the land. The RIB nosed gently in among the stones of the small beach.

Sam jumped out as Niall steadied the boat, keeping its bow pointed in to shore. He handed me out over the thwart and began passing Sam their packs and gear, and what seemed like an endless supply of shopping bags. The pebbly beach was nestled into the side of a promontory, which partially sheltered the anchorage from the north. Further along to the east the beach disappeared into rough grassland where dunes reached the sea, and a small jetty ran out into deeper water. The sparsely grassed dunes separated the beach from the view inland, and all I could see beyond them was a couple of trees and the glimpse of a grey roof.

Scanning the scene I came back round to the seashore. Niall had emptied the boat and edged it down to the eastern end of the pebbly shore, where he was busy hauling it up onto a grassy slope above the high tide line. Sam eyed the pile of bags at his feet, then lifted his fingers to his mouth and whistled. Shouts greeted this sound and I spun round to see figures pouring through a gap in the dunes.

At first it seemed a crowd of people had emerged from nowhere, but as I trotted behind them through the dunes I realised there were no more than a dozen. In short order they had the bags decanted into the kitchen of the building I had seen from the beach, and a couple of them were busy re-heating multiple packs of fried rice, noodles, meat and vegetables. By the time Niall jogged up from the beach the tables were set and all of us were crowding onto benches and helping ourselves to food.

So much for another rest day. Niall and Sam may have taken some time off, but the dirt-smeared T-shirts and trousers of several of the team suggested they'd carried on working while the boss was away. I wasn't very hungry, and soon found myself pushed back from the table, leaning against the wall as I listened to the hum of voices around me.

Slowly the others worked their way through the food, and two of the younger ones cleared away the debris and began washing up in the kitchen. Niall leaned forward with his elbows on the table, like the patriarch of a large and unruly family, and called for quiet. He got it, more-or-less, in only a few minutes, and the two from the kitchen poked their heads out to hear what he had to say.

"I'd like to introduce you all to Cas Longmore," he said, gesturing towards me. Everyone was already looking my way – maybe as a stranger I was the most interesting thing they'd seen that day, but the attention seemed to be friendly and I smiled back at them all. "Cas is Sam's Mum, but of course you've all heard of her as the person who discovered the evidence which led to my dig in north Mull last summer."

"Your ship burial." shouted one of the young ones from the kitchen doorway.

Niall flushed red under his tan. The colour seeped up under his shirt collar and made his face blaze for a moment. Then he shrugged. "It serves me right for speculating before the fact." He turned to me again and explained, "I got rather over-excited when I first found you in that void in Mull – where we eventually found the second chess piece."

"Rescued me," I said, smiling at him.

"Well, yes, thank you. Although it was really Sam who rescued you. I just happened to be the lucky one who was along for the ride. As a result, I had first dibs to excavate a completely unknown site. There were a number of clues pointing to a boat, and one of the most exciting possibilities was a boat burial, which has never been recorded before in this part of Scotland. The nearest comparable site is on Ardnamurchan, a very exciting site where a high ranking Viking burial was found in a boat-shaped pit, complete with grave goods including a sword. It was probably too much to hope that our site was of similar quality, but I was really looking forward to unravelling its story.

"Unfortunately, I spoke a little too freely to the local press. They ran a story about the Viking chieftain buried on

Mull, and I was hounded by people wanting to know if a treasure like Sutton Hoo had been found in the Inner Hebrides. It's very difficult to get the public interested in the minutiae of archaeology – and the Ardnamurchan site had rather stolen our thunder."

Niall ran his hand through his hair, looking harassed. "It's a constant wonder to me, the way people mix up Vikings and Anglo Saxons. It's as if they have no idea of history at all."

I hoped I was imagining the look he threw at me as he said this. I know a lot more about the Middle Ages in Scotland than I used to, thanks to the Calgary Chess Queen, but nowhere near enough to impress a proper archaeologist.

"Anyway, at the end of the dig all we found were a couple of iron-stained rivet-like patches in the fill, half a warder (confirming that it was indeed very likely that your chess piece, Cas, came from the same site) and some lumps and bits, some of which turned out to be human bone. It's by no means certain there ever was a boat in that place, and even if there was, there's no way to tell whether it was a deliberate burial, a shipwreck, or even an upturned boat used as a house.

"Although we cobbled together a story based on the site, Cas, plus your find and the probable set of scales dredged up by a fisherman a generation before in the same waters, we really didn't find enough evidence to tell the full story. A bit of carved ivory and the excavation documents, while of great interest to others in the field, did nothing to fulfil the expectations of the press, and I'm afraid I've rather lost my credibility with them."

Niall smiled at me and put his hand into his pocket. "This seems as good a moment as any to give you this," he said. He pulled out the usual silk handkerchief, opened it out and handed me the Calgary Chess Queen. I held her up and looked her in the eye. She didn't look especially pleased to see me, but I was familiar with that superior expression. I certainly hadn't expected to have her in my hands again.

"This isn't a copy, is it?" I said.

"No, this is the real thing. The museum finished with its exhibition of last year's finds, and our little collection wasn't deemed important enough for them to hold onto it. There were only the three pieces: your queen, found in the sand at Calgary; Mr MacInnes' object, dragged up in his fishing net and now postulated to be part of a set of scales; and the warder, found at the dig site. Because they weren't found together they couldn't be treated as linked pieces, even though the case we made out was good.

"The rules here in Scotland say that all finds belong to the crown, not the finder. After examination they are offered to any museums that want them, and the finder is paid the true value of the piece. It's a good system – makes it fairly unlikely that finders will pocket important finds and not report them. Generally, it's local museums that most want items found in the local area, so the law of Treasure Trove helps to keep objects in the general area where they were found.

"In this case, there were no local museums interested in the piece. The Metropolitan Museum could have made a case to keep it, along with the other pieces found at the dig site, but they weren't especially excited either. Because your piece was found out of context, it's of limited archaeological value. So I made a bid on behalf of Mull Museum, and it was accepted."

He smiled at me.

"The Calgary Queen no longer belongs to you. In the meantime she forms part of the assemblage I dug last year, if only by association. I'm responsible for her until my write-up is finished, at which point she will have to make her way to the museum in Tobermory. Until that moment arrives, I thought you might enjoy having her in your possession again."

"I thought single items found out of context didn't count as treasure trove, unless they were especially valuable?" I hefted the little figure in my hand, surprised all over again at how heavy she was.

"That's true, south of the border. Here in Scotland the

law is different."

I stood eye-to-eye with the figure for a moment, then handed her round so everyone could take a look. She might not have been deemed important enough for the Met to hold onto her, but that didn't stop every archaeologist in the room taking an interest. I guess it's not often you get to hold a real piece of the nation's history, albeit one whose story remains largely untold. Eventually, she made her way back to me and I tucked her into the pocket of my jeans.

The discussion broke up for a moment, as mugs of tea and coffee were passed round, and then Niall took the floor again. Quickly he introduced the others to me, and I took stock of his team. Joint team leader, and in charge of the students who were doing the bulk of the excavation work, was 'Big John' Duncan, a mediaeval specialist from a university in the Midlands. He had been responsible for sourcing most of the funding that paid for the dig, and the team of excitable young archaeology students came mostly from his courses at the university.

John was exactly as his nickname suggested, a tall, well-built man. With his sandy beard and ready laugh, he looked exactly as you might imagine a Viking chieftain to look, although his accent was Midlands through and through. He was working side by side with Niall as joint team leaders, although he modestly told me that Niall was really in charge, to the vociferous denials of his students.

As well as supervision and training of his young team, John shared responsibility with Tim Rigby for producing geophysical evidence to inform the diggers; Tim came and went at weekly intervals, as he was also advising at another dig on the mainland. Niall assured me I'd meet Tim in the next day or two, as he was due back at any time.

"We'll need Tim if we find anything at Annaid."

John nodded. "You could say, we need Tim first to see if there's anything to find," he added.

Niall inclined his head to John, who introduced the student members of his team: Elisabeta Adrianova, Irene Stewart, Rick Mason, Lily Bonner, Louise Ferguson and

Amanda MacLean. "We should have had another pair, but they got the last minute chance to participate in a dig in Morocco. Who could resist that? The irony is that there's been an unseasonal low over North Africa all week, and we've probably had warmer weather than they have."

Everyone laughed and one of the girls spoke up. "You got the best," she said, and the others agreed. The girl spoke in a distinctive Eastern European accent (Polish? Russian? Maybe, but I'm not very good at identifying accents). She must be Elisabeta. I wondered which of the other girls was which.

"Sam, of course, you know," said Niall, indicating my son, who rose and took a bow. "That's the whole team except for Annette. Annette's our site recorder, both for photographs and mapping. Where is she? I didn't see her at dinner."

"I'm here." The low voice came from behind me. I turned round and saw the figure of a woman silhouetted in the doorway. "I've been asleep. I didn't feel like dinner. What are we discussing?"

She moved into the room and I saw that she was lovely: a tall red-head of the kind whose skin is like milk. She wore cargo trousers and a man's shirt with rolled-up sleeves as though they were haute couture. The shirt was buttoned just a little too low, showing a glimpse of cleavage and more of that perfect skin, and when she moved her hips swayed slightly. I wondered whether she was conscious of the effect. She sashayed across the room and held out her hand to me.

"Hello, I'm Annette Wheeler."

"Cas Longmore," I said, feeling dowdy, middle-aged and distinctly ordinary as the glorious creature leaned over me. "I'm pleased to meet you."

Those perfect breasts rose and fell as she looked down at me. I held my breath. She released my hand and straightened up. "Likewise," she said. Then she reached past me and ruffled Sam's hair. "Hello, pretty boy," she purred. Sam flinched, then became utterly still.

Annette turned her attention on Niall. It was like a searchlight being switched off: it almost felt cooler in the room now that I wasn't under the spotlight of her gaze. "I've finished today's drawings. What have you planned for tomorrow?"

Now Niall looked for a moment like a rabbit in the headlights of an oncoming car, but he soon recovered his savoir faire. "I intend to spend the morning going over all the evidence gathered so far. Cas will want to see it, and John and I could do with some conference time before we decide on our next move. Am I right in saying nothing new has turned up today?"

A chorus of "No, nothing..." greeted his question. Niall looked at me, and then back up at Annette. Interestingly, he hadn't stood up when she came in. Not every man does these days, but it surprised me nonetheless. From behind I thought her body language was a little tense, too. Niall addressed his students again. "We'll get you guys to finish off trench three tomorrow, you should be able to wrap and re-cover it before lunch. Then you can take some time off. John and I are going to take Cas down to Annaid to look the place over, decide what we want Tim to do when he gets back."

"I can tell you what's at Annaid," said Annette. She pulled out a spare chair and sat down in it, crossing her legs elegantly.

"Annette, we've been through this," started Niall, but she interrupted him, sitting forward and fiercely grasping his forearm as he made to stand.

"Listen to me. All those dusty old reports saying that 'annaid' means an old church, and it's just a place where the church building got moved somewhere different, but the old place was remembered. How many of those places have any real evidence of buildings? They're always isolated, out-of-the-way places, nowhere near any sites of habitation. Maybe hermitage sites. Maybe. But how many of those sites have wells or springs?

"Niall, you know as well as I do that wells and springs

mean the Old Religion. Annats are places of the Goddess. I'm sure of it. And this one on Lismore is right in the middle of a whole pile of archaeology, from duns and brochs to old farm buildings. About the only thing that hasn't ever been found there is a church or monastic building. There's even a spring. This one has even kept its ancient spelling of Annaid, when nearly all the others in Scotland have become Annat.

"Come on, Niall, you know it makes sense. Even Samuel Johnson confirmed that the Goddess was worshipped here."

Niall eased his arm out from under her hand. I could see the marks of her nails, at first white where she had gripped so hard, then red as his circulation reasserted itself. He rubbed his arm and leaned back in his chair.

"Samuel Johnson?" I said. "The dictionary Samuel Johnson?"

"Yes." Annette turned her intense regard onto me, then back to Niall. "There's documentary proof that he and Boswell visited a water temple of the Goddess Annait, whom he compared to a goddess of the same name in the Middle East."

"That was reported apocryphally in the parish writings of one district. Johnson himself never wrote anything about it. There's no proof he ever made such a visit. Even the documentation we do have refers to 'Annait, an ancient site of worship'. Nothing there to support the idea of widespread Goddess worship in Scotland. As for the Annaid here, it has probably kept to its proper spelling and pronunciation because the Gaelic language held on longer on Lismore than the mainland and larger islands hereabouts."

Annette opened her mouth as if to speak, but Niall rode over her. As he continued, she frowned and began to inspect her perfectly groomed fingernails. Her face was calm, but one foot swung as she listened.

"It's an accident of history that Lismore maintained its community intact for longer than almost anywhere else during the clearances, and as a result kept its language alive as well. I do agree that names can tell us something about the people who originally lived in these places, and I'd give your ideas a little more credence if there were any other local names that suggested associations with the Goddess."

Annette perked up. "What about Sloc a' Bhrighide? That's only just up the coast from Annaid."

"Bride's Rock. Okay, I'll give you that one, but it's not enough. I can't overturn the entire agreed history of the Inner Hebrides to suit your theory. There has to be evidence."

"All the evidence you need is in the name. I'm named for the goddess Annait, and so are all her places." Annette gave up the pretence of calmness and jumped to her feet. She marched up and down in front of Niall, gesticulating as she spoke. "It seems obvious to me. Why is so hard to convince you?"

"Annette, I'd love you to have your day. Finding evidence for goddess worship in Scotland would really set the cat among the pigeons, and I know how much you'd enjoy the pandemonium it would cause, but it must wait until we find the proof."

"You'll find it here on Lismore. Right there at Annaid. The time is right. I can feel it."

Annette spun on her heel and marched out of the hall. I took a second look, just to make sure she wasn't wearing high heeled shoes: her sway was exactly what you'd expect to see on the catwalk. She disappeared into the darkness and we looked at one other. I became aware that we'd all been holding our breath. I wasn't the only one affected by that striking presence. The students began to murmur among themselves and I commandeered Niall's attention.

"Annette said 'Bride's Rock.' What has that got to do with goddesses?"

"Sloc a Bhrighide," Niall repeated the Gaelic name. "Meaning 'the rock of Brigid' or, in English, 'Bride's Rock'. Brigid is an ancient Irish character, part myth and part historical figure. She was one of the earliest monastic founders, back in the early days when women were valued equally with men in the church. The monastic Brigid may well have been a real person, but she's also associated with the mythical Brigid, one of Ireland's tutelary goddesses."

I nodded, but I was still puzzled. "I've heard of Saint Brigid. I didn't know she had anything to do with Scotland."

"This part of Scotland was settled from Ireland, especially the islands which became part of the district known as Dal Riata. Scottish Gaelic arose from Irish roots, and no doubt they brought their myths with them and applied them to the landscape. So a feature named after Brigid might suggest an association with the Irish goddess of the same name, although there's no possible way to know for sure."

Niall looked around him. The small crowd had thinned, as some of the team had already gone to their tents. "I'm for bed," he said, rising to his feet. "Cas, I'll show you to your tent. In a couple of days Lou and Mandy are heading to Tim's other dig, and you can have their tent, but for the next night or two you'll have to put up with Sam."

"You'll be all right," said Sam, grinning. "I don't snore."

"That's not what I remember," I told him, as we walked out into the evening air.

The sea air and good company had tired me out and I fell asleep easily. Later I found myself standing knee-deep in surf at Huna Cove, shading my eyes from the setting sun: my own special haven, my private place, the little piece of New Zealand that I carry round in my head (and heart).

The low sun cast long shadows over the beach from the stones at the water's edge. Small waves washed in, each cresting in a froth of burning silver. A cool wind whipped my nightdress around my thighs, but the back of my neck was still hot from afternoon sun, and beads of sweat clung to my brow. As the sun sank lower the water turned deep scarlet and the waves seemed to move more and more slowly, as if the sea had turned to treacle.

Behind me came a sound, deep and guttural, almost below hearing: like the groan of a distant land slip, or the deep earth's notice of an imminent tremor. I turned and saw a figure, limned in light but still somehow indistinct, hanging in the air. It spoke, in a voice like the earthquake: "Cassandra, what are you?"

I shivered in my dream and wrapped my nightdress around myself, only to discover I was naked. I hugged myself and realised my chest was smooth and flat, my hips narrow and boyish. I looked down at myself and saw that I had a penis. Panicking, I turned away from the numinous figure, clutching at those unexpected extra parts of me. The sun went down into a sea of blood and its last rays shot into my eyes, making me stumble backwards, blinking away hot tears. Suddenly it was dark. I choked on the surge of acid in my throat and coughed.

Immediately I was awake in the small tent, with Sam leaning over me. My arm hurt where he'd poked me, hard.

"Sorry, Mum," he said. "You were snoring and then you started mumbling. It woke me up."

"Thanks," I muttered, not very thankfully. What a disturbing dream. I suppose I should be grateful Sam had woken me. Huna Cove is my sanctuary of the mind, always tranquil and calming even when the wind is high and the tide surges against the shore. I'd never dreamed of it like that before.

Some of the imagery I could understand – that gleaming, blood-red sea was the evil twin of the golden plate of ocean I'd sat by yesterday, watching the seal and the otter – but as for the cross-gender images, they were much more disturbing.

I hadn't dreamed myself in a boy's body since I was a young adolescent, when maleness had seemed to be such a great mystery, and I dreamed several times that my budding female bits had metamorphosed into the quintessential male possession. Every new farm hand, every male visitor to the farm had to unwittingly succumb to being mentally undressed by me, as I tried to imagine my way to an understanding of my own feelings and the differences between men and women.

I suppose that now I am in a kind of second adolescence

– suddenly released from the strictures of a loveless marriage, free to imagine whatever relationships I wish. No wonder my subconscious mind is jumping through hoops. I wriggled over onto my side and forced my eyes shut.

5

I picked up a couple of mugs left over from breakfast and handed them to Sam in the kitchen, while Niall spread papers and maps all over the tables. Big John wandered in and leaned over his shoulder, pointing to a place on the map. The two of them conferred quietly for a moment, then John wandered off again.

"We should plan to be ready to leave about eleven," he said as he went.

"Thanks," said Niall. He looked up and beckoned me over. "Come and see what we're up to." He pointed to the big map of Lismore that he and John had been bent over a moment before. "Here's the village of Achnacroish – you know that that means?"

"Field of the Cross," I said. "That's an easy one."

"Indeed. That gives you the first clue there could be a religious site around here, although to be honest a cross doesn't always mean a monastery. Could be a market or chapel site, a location sacred in pre-Christian times or even just a crossroads, but there's been a long tradition here on Lismore that Achnacroish is an important religious site.

"Down on the coast is the village of Port Moluag, named for the founder of the monastic lineage which centred on Lismore. Over here," his finger stabbed at a point a few centimetres further inland. "This is the site of the present church, which is all that remains of the Cathedral of the Isles, for which Lismore was famous in the Middle Ages."

"So that confirms you've got a really important site here?"

Niall shook his head. "It's not as simple as that. We know the present church consists of the choir of the old cathedral, and that geophys has found evidence of buried walls and pillars, confirming the existence of the larger building. There are a lot of graves around that area as well, but it's separated from the modern village by a slight rise and an expanse of fields, which are mostly now used for sheep. My…our surmise has been that there was a monastic site here before the cathedral was ever constructed, and some test pits done a few years ago suggested it might be in the area to the east of the church."

"A cathedral?" I asked. "I've never heard about anything like that here."

"Lismore was the heart of its own diocese, and Port Moluag was the site of the cathedral. There's one wing of it left standing, and it's used as the present Parish church. It was never a well-populated parish, but it had a cathedral nonetheless."

Niall moved further down the table to where some black and white photographs had been laid out. "Here's an aerial view of the area, taken during the very dry summer four years ago."

I remember that summer. It was the last holiday I spent together with Sam and his father, a few months before the process of separation and all its rows, insults and petty squabbles began. The weather had been gloriously dry and warm for the whole five weeks of our stay – utterly unlike the usual damp, midgy Mull experience. Life hadn't seemed too bad despite my differences with Drew. Sam hadn't hit adolescence yet. We went fishing with Ewan, and Drew made a fool of himself demanding the big boat, showing off his wealth and assuming that whatever he wanted, money would buy it. I did not miss that man at all.

Niall indicated a pale marking on the aerial photograph. "That's the vallum. You see how it follows the line of the ridge, then turns east and disappears under the village houses?"

"Vallum?" I asked.

"The boundary ditch and bank marking out the monastic precincts. Changes in the subsoil, such as filled-in ditches or eroded banks, affect the drainage and fertility of the soil, and that can show up in summer photographs as crop marks: lighter or darker lines indicating the layout of hidden features beneath. See how the church is just outside the main line of the vallum to the west, and the vallum bulges out around it. It was probably extended to take in the site of the church, which makes me think that may have been built later than the original monastery."

"Is that usual?" I asked. "Aren't monasteries always laid out to the same plan?"

"I wish," said Niall ruefully. "That would make my life much easier."

"I thought we knew all about how monasteries are laid out – church, cloisters, refectory, dormitory and so on. I didn't think there was that much left to discover."

"Oh, no, here in Scotland it's all to play for. We have an idea of the types of buildings that might be found in a monastery, but there's no overarching plan. It's not like the Romans, who were touchingly predictable in the layout of their forts and fortlets. Monks seem to have had ideas of their own. And it's made more difficult by the fact that the really famous monastic sites, like Iona, are so precious that virtually no archaeological exploration is allowed there."

He fished about among the papers on the table and pulled out a tourist's map of Iona. There was a photo of the Abbey on the front page, and inside it folded out to reveal a map of Lismore with interesting places marked. He laid it alongside an aerial photograph that was clearly of the same site, with some markings picked out in felt pen.

"On Iona you can see the vallum on aerial views, and everyone knows where the big buildings like the abbey and the nunnery are, but if you look more closely at the aerial photo you can see the whole site is criss-crossed with little lines and patches. It's nigh on impossible to imagine what they might be, let alone what period of Iona's development they belong to. And no excavation is allowed. The site is being preserved for the future, and they don't want curious archaeologists digging holes in it."

"How frustrating for you," I said sympathetically.

"You have no idea."

"What about the new site on Mull?" I asked Niall. "You seemed pretty confident when you were showing me and Sam around that."

"Oh, well. That was half knowledge and half bullshit," acknowledged Niall, smiling up at me through his fringe as he swept the hair off his face and tucked it behind his ears. (How many times have I seen him make that gesture? It seems curiously feminine and I wonder why, if it annoys him so much, he doesn't simply get it cut.)

"We can make some sensible guesses about what went on at the site. There must have been somewhere to sleep, somewhere to prepare food, somewhere to play. They probably grew crops, kept some animals, made beer. If it was a big enough monastery, maybe they scraped skins or make parchment, ground inks, wove cloth. Large communities were probably quite self-sufficient.

"A tiny community would have consisted only of a few monks, perhaps the magic number of thirteen – a leader and twelve followers, believed to be the perfect number as it matches Jesus and his apostles. But a really big community would have had a whole raft of supporting personnel, many of them with families, so it could look more like a large village than an isolated community of men. That's why it's helpful to find burials. A cemetery containing only adult males provides a completely different picture of the type of occupation than one which contains bodies of both sexes and a range of ages."

"What do you think you're looking at here on Lismore?"

"Take a look at the geophys results." I obediently moved round to the other side of the table. Wiping his hands, Sam joined us from the kitchen. "Yes, let's. I've been doing nothing but trotting round behind you doing your errands since we arrived here. I'd like to see some real archaeology."

"Sam, don't be rude," I exclaimed, but Niall was laughing.

"Enough cheek from you," he said. "A few days' spade

and trowel work will sort you out. How do you fancy wet-sieving the pile of fill the girls dug out yesterday, while you were swanning round Tobermory with me?"

"No boss, sorry boss, won't happen again," said Sam, miming tugging at a forelock. "I'll do whatever you ask – please don't make me do wet-sieving."

"I should make you do it, to prove I mean business," growled Niall. "I made my first proper find sorting through buckets of mud that someone else had already looked over. That's what a proper apprenticeship is about: getting your hands dirty and your back sore, with no guarantee of any reward at the end of it."

"Anything you say, boss," said Sam, resting his head on Niall's shoulder and looking up at him with his endearing puppy face on.

"Get off me," said Niall, pushing him away. "I'm showing your Mum the geophys."

Sam danced round behind us and ended up looking over my shoulder as Niall began to point out features on the array of printouts. I couldn't get over what had just happened. Obviously Sam didn't just admire Niall, he also liked him – liked him enough to tease him, with confidence that Niall would give as good as he got. I hadn't seen Sam so relaxed with anyone before. Is this what he's like with his school friends?

He didn't have anything like such an easy relationship with his father, who always seemed to be looking for something to complain about, usually so he could blame me (the convenient, available target) or the school (wasting vast amounts of Drew's money, and this is all they can produce at the end of it).

It was nice to see Sam acting confidently with his employer, but I hoped he wouldn't get so cocky that he failed to take full advantage of the opportunity he'd been offered here. It certainly looked as though Sam's interest in archaeology was continuing, but if he wanted a career in the field then he needed to show he could muck in with the rest of them and treat every job seriously.

I stood and looked at the sheets Niall was spreading out on the table. A bewildering series of patterns in black, white and grey, zigzagged, blotted and sprawled their way across the paper. One sheet looked like static on a TV screen, the next like the crazed imaginings of a monochrome hippy on acid. I groaned. "How on earth do you ever make sense of this?"

"I'm glad you asked that," said Niall. "John, how about you help me out here?"

It was Big John's turn to grumble. "Do I have to?" he said, histrionically. Sam giggled and Niall smiled. "Just tell us what Tim would say."

"Well, um," began John. "What Tim would say is…"

"What Tim would say is, step out of the way and let the expert speak."

Everyone turned, to see a slight figure standing in the doorway. "Tim, welcome back," said John, sounded extremely relieved. Tim made his way to the table and, shunting onlookers aside by sweeping his arms apart, beckoned me to his side after a brief introduction by Niall, and began to show me how to make sense out of apparent chaos.

"Take this one first," he said, indicating what seemed to be a picture of a topographical landscape, covered with little peaks and ridges. "This is a magnetometry plot of our main site, here on Lismore. We're looking for anywhere human beings have disturbed the subsoil, by digging into it for farming, pits, ditches, clearing ground for building. All these things change the magnetic characteristics of the soil, and we can detect the anomalies and rapidly build up a picture of what lies beneath our feet. Here," and he pointed to a distinct line curving round the right quadrant of the picture.

"This is probably the vallum, the boundary ditch of the monastery, if indeed we have found our monastery. Of course, it could be some other kind of ditch or bank feature. We have to dig it to be sure."

Niall nodded agreement. "Geophysical survey is one of

the first things we do, if we can afford Tim and his team. It tells us where to dig and, sometimes more importantly, can stop us wasting our time digging where there's nothing to find."

"Now, if you look at this one," Tim pushed the magnetometry sheet aside and pulled another in front of me, this one looking more like a maze of straight lines, interlocking cubes and rectangles. It reminded me of a picture I'd seen in one of the physics textbooks I'd proofread, of crystals forming in a super cooled liquid. The whole sheet seemed covered with the little squares.

"This is the resistivity plot of a dig I surveyed last year in York. Electrical resistivity is really good for picking up buried structures, such as stone walls and foundations. This mess represents hundreds of years of building, layer upon layer of stone buildings over the history of the city.

"If you compare it to this," bringing over another page to sit side by side with the crystal lattice. "This is the combined data from magnetometry and resistivity surveys of a site on Rathlin Island, in the sea lanes between Scotland and Ireland. It's almost certainly an early monastic site." Tim traced the outline of a more-or-less oval boundary, and a number of roundish shapes attached to the inside of the boundary line. The centre of the oval held some indistinct marks, but none of the lines were straight.

"Classic vallum with monastic cells lining the inner bank. Now, this one," shunting all the pages aside and beckoning to Niall, who handed over a new page from the trestle beside him, "is part of the resistivity plot of our current site. It more-or-less matches the area covered by the magnetometry plot we were looking at a few minutes ago. You'll notice that there's no sign of the vallum. That's because it's a ditch – it shows up loud and clear under magnetometry, but its electrical signature is negligible and so it doesn't show up at all in the resistivity plot. But here you can see some curved lines, some straight, and a corner or two."

When he pointed them out, I tried to convince myself I

could see some apparent pattern to the dark lines, but there were far fewer of them than on the York sheet Tim had shown me. "Are they buildings, then?"

"Absolutely right. Stone shows up very well under the resistivity scan, so whenever you see a clear signature like that, with the kinds of straight lines or corners that rarely occur in nature, you can be pretty sure you've got some kind of structure."

"Are the round shapes cells, and the square ones storage?" asked Sam. "They're all quite small. How can you tell the square ones aren't kelp burning kilns? They wouldn't be part of the monastery at all."

"Good question," said Tim. Niall nodded sagely in the background. Sam looked pleased with himself.

"You're right that if these straight lines represent structures they're too small for major monastic buildings such as refectory or infirmary. It's possible they're storage facilities, or small workshops, but equally they're close enough to the sea to represent kelp-burning kilns. The kelp industry was at its peak in the eighteenth century. It mostly closed down at the end of the Napoleonic Wars, although in some of the islands it continued until the beginning of the twentieth century, supplying iodine to the glass making industry. To sort out the dates of these features, we are going to have to dig."

"Hooray," said Ree, dancing in the doorway.

"Yes." Tim smiled at her enthusiasm. "Get your trowels out; it's your turn to shine."

"So, how do you tell where the bodies are buried?" I asked. Tim, John, Niall and Sam all laughed. I felt stupid, but Tim patted my hand. "Actually, it's a good question," he went on. "None of our geophysical survey methods are any good for finding bodies, although they do sometimes show up concentrations of metal grave goods. If the body's buried in a lead coffin or a stone kist, then it's Christmas time for us. We get a big rectangular blob that shouts out to be excavated. Sometimes we can see in the magnetometry where a large area of ground has been disturbed for a cemetery, but that's more likely to happen near a very large settlement, such as a city. We do think it might be worth putting in a test pit here," indicating an area just inside the vallum line on the magnetometry sheet. "I'd suggest this area is our best bet for a possible cemetery associated with the monks, but I wouldn't want to place any actual money on it."

Big John grinned, pulled a ten pound note out of his pocket and slammed it down on the table in front of Tim. "I have a good feeling about this one," he said.

Niall took out another and laid it side by side with John's. "My money's on the other side of the church," he said. "But I agree we need to eliminate this area first. First test pit goes in tomorrow, while we take Cas for a look at Annaid. Maybe one of us will be buying the other's drinks when we get back."

Both men looked down at Tim, who spread his hands wide and shrugged. "I'm not wasting my money betting on anything, though I'll be happy to take the credit if the site turns out to be stuffed full of bones."

"And if there's nothing there, you'll claim you said so all along?"

"Exactement."

6

The small car bounced and jolted over the rough stone surface, tossing us against each other and almost crowning tall John against the roof. I twisted round and looked out the back window. The Land Rover would have made easy work of this track, but I guess the needs of the main dig site had to take precedence. I grimaced at Sam and he grinned back, wanly. He was definitely looking a bit green, and looked quickly away from me and out of the window. The car slewed round a corner and across a tiny culverted stream, and the coast came into view again.

John drove us down the last few hundred yards, across an ancient cattle grid, and into what must once have been a farmyard, now knee high in flowering weeds. I climbed gratefully from the car and stretched. Sam stood a few feet away, bent forward and breathing deeply, his face still pale with a spot of colour high on each cheek. Niall and John headed straight across the flat yard to a fallen gate and clambered over it into a boggy looking meadow. I stretched again, yawned, and looked around me. The car was parked (in the midst of a riot of dandelions) in front of a terrace of three buildings.

The left hand house was the most substantial, and in the best condition – it looked as though it had seen recent repair, and might even (possibly) be liveable. The centre house had a hole in the roof, with a tree growing out of it, and in front of the house a pile of smashed tiles entangled in greenery showed how water and seeds had managed to gain access to the roof timbers. The house nearest to me was present only as a suggestion of its former self.

From the end wall of the middle house, a couple of stone piers protruded, front and back, with a suggestion of a window in the broken end of the front wall. A small pile of rubble hinted at the end wall of the cottage, but there was not enough to account for the whole house. I guessed that at some time in the past stone had been robbed, perhaps for field boundaries or other buildings on the island. It wasn't even possible to guess whether the damage was decades old, or more recent.

Turning round I saw Sam straightening up, his colour already much improved. Beyond him, screened by some sycamores that looked the worse for exposure to sea winds, was a low hill that blocked out any view of the sea. I walked through the farmyard and manoeuvred myself over the broken gate, following Niall and John. As I picked my way across the boggy patch, looking for drier ground, I saw that the low hill to the left came to an end, and the pasture led away south-westward, until it ended at a seaweed and rock strewn beach.

A tiny patch of yellowish sand was lapped by the gentlest of waves, in the lee of a line of rocks which projected the slope of the hill into the sea. Another jumble of rocks on the northern edge of the strand completed the picture. It was a miniature harbour, just the right size for a single boat, drawn up on the sand, or a single small family of beach-lovers.

I clambered across the rocks and seaweed, pulled off my shoes and socks and rolled up my trousers. The water was cool, but not as cold as expected. The tide looked to be on its way in, and the shallow patch of sand was warming the wavelets as they played across it. I turned round and looked back towards the gable end of the farmhouse, but it was tucked away, out of sight behind the hill. The whole scene was pleasingly intimate, with a feeling of peacefulness and serenity.

This must have been a lovely place to live, the house site sheltered from the cold north and east by the bulk of Lismore, from the southerly blow by the shoulder of the hill, and with its own perfect harbour waiting patiently for visitors. Everything here felt domestic, from the cluster of three dwellings and the tiny harbour to the small flat pasture with a little ruined stone building (house? pigsty?) backed into the shelter of a low cliff. Further inland, the hill slopes stretched away up to the road we had driven down, and I could see the outline of a fank on the shoulder of the hill.

Niall and John stood by the fank, looking in my direction. Niall was waving his arms about, while John made notes on his clipboard. I guessed they were mapping out the scene below them, looking for clues of former occupancy. Sam headed up to join them. As he reached the two men, and turned to look where they were looking, I noticed that he was mid-way in height between the two of them. Big John, of course, was exactly as his name suggested, but even Niall was at least average height for a man. While I hadn't been looking, Sam had grown again. I found myself wondering when he was going to stop. He had matched me in height a year ago, a milestone that somehow passed us both by while we were dealing with the discovery of the Calgary Chess Queen, and a few other things besides.

There were not many milestones left in our shared relationship. Soon now, much sooner than I'd bargained for, he was going to be finishing school, leaving home for good (not just for term time) and charting his own course on the choppy seas of adulthood. I thought I'd come to terms with that last summer, but suddenly realised I was still as anxious as I had been a year ago. Perhaps that's the way it works. I'll keep worrying about him no matter how old he gets. I just have to make sure he doesn't know how much I worry.

The three men were scanning the horizon and sharing an earnest discussion. I began to pick my way across the lower field toward the stone structure that abutted the cliff face. As I came closer my first impression was vindicated – it looked far too well made to be a mere pigsty. Three walls of finely meshed stones rose to a height of about four feet. The fourth wall of the building made use of the cliff behind. A jumble of stones in the middle of the structure told the story of a partial wall collapse.

I couldn't see any sign of roof tile among the stones, so

perhaps it wasn't a house. Anyway, it was a bit small. Apart from the doorway there was only one other apparent opening, a low point in the end wall which perhaps represented a window.

The building measured about eight feet long by around four feet deep: nothing more than a single room built out from the cliff. I was starting to push my way through the doorway, and leaned slightly on the lintel as I ducked to go in. A cracking sound warned me and I jumped back, barely in time before another couple of stones detached themselves from the upper wall of the structure. I heard a yell from up the hill, and within moments the three men had arrived at my side. I brushed dust from my shoulders and braced myself to receive some masculine sympathy.

"What the hell do you think you're doing?" Niall's voice cut through my pleasant fantasy. I straightened my spine and looked him in the eye.

"Looking at some potential archaeology," I stated grandly.

"Ruining it more like," retorted Niall, going far redder with anger than he'd done with embarrassment the day before. He opened his mouth to say more, but thought better of it. His shoulders slumped. "I don't know why I bother," he said.

John made no comment, but his sidelong look spoke volumes as he brushed past me to look into the doorway I'd vacated. Sam patted my shoulder as he went past. A rather patronising pat, I felt. As if I was the only person who didn't know what I'd done wrong.

Oh, hell, I admit it. I do know I shouldn't go poking around old places just because I'm curious. And as for doing it in front of Niall – I well remember him ranting at length last year about people who remove finds from the ground, thereby destroying their archaeological context and with it any chance of working out the story of the object. He'd come very close to implying I'd done that with the Calgary Chess Queen, albeit unwittingly.

I suppose I should count myself lucky he hadn't had a go

at me for falling into the void from which he'd rescued me last summer. For all that I'd 'discovered' an unknown mediaeval site on Mull, he could quite justifiably have accused me of poking my nose in where it didn't belong. And here I've just gone and done it again.

While I was beating myself up, Niall and John had eased themselves into the middle of the building, stirring up a cloud of dust and a small rumble as stone shifted. Hmphh. Apparently it's perfectly okay when archaeologists disturb the site.

"Look here." John indicated a much larger stone forming part of a side wall of the structure.

"Yes, definitely," said Niall.

"Definitely what?" asked Sam, saving me the bother of having to ask the same question. Niall and John were obviously used to finishing each other's thoughts, without even bothering to speak them.

"Possible standing stone reused in a later structure," said John, pushing his hand in behind another large stone, this one leaning against the cliff face. "This one looks more like a fallen lintel. Hang on," grunting, "there's a void here, Niall."

He withdrew his hand again and the two of them looked at each other.

"Definitely need to get Tim down here for some proper geophys. There was another standing stone used in the fank up the hill. Be interesting to see if there are any alignments here. And this ruin bears further investigation."

"What do you reckon? Get the team down tomorrow, if they've cleaned up on site today?"

"Yes. Get some preliminary mapping done, and make a plan of action. Annette can record. It's a pity we no longer have the photos of the 1996 expedition." He looked at me and Sam. "In 1996 an archaeological field team recorded all the visible features on the southern quadrant of Lismore, and published a report on the structures they found. Some of them, like the two duns up the road and the abandoned farmstead, are already well known, but we think they described other features that we might like to have had a second look at.

"Unfortunately, something went wrong in the data storage process, and records of the area went missing, including a database of photographs that might even have included this structure. It would have been useful to compare today's landscape with one over a decade older, but we'll just have to start from scratch now."

John spoke up. "I think this large one has slipped over from the end wall. It's not in situ. Might be interesting to take a quick look at the void behind it?"

He and Niall eyed each other. I could almost hear the cogs whirring as they made their mutual calculations. "I agree. Sam, step back a little. We're going to shift this to the left, and I don't want it to end up on your foot."

They moved the lintel stone sideways with great care, and we all held our breaths until they set it down again. Niall reached into one of his trouser pockets and pulled out a tiny torch. It lit up the inside of the void with a narrow but surprisingly bright beam of light. Niall muttered to himself as he played it round the space inside: "Bigger than you'd think. Must be formed from a natural cave. Big enough for a cell, maybe?"

"Maybe," said John. "Could support your idea about a monastic presence down here. We definitely need to excavate this. What's that at the back?"

The torch beam came to rest on a dark patch on the back wall of the 'cave', about three feet above the ground. "Shelf or recess of some kind," Niall confirmed. "There's something there. Here, hold this."

He gave the torch to John, who obediently aimed it at the dark hole. Sam and I crowded each other in the entrance to the void, trying to see and failing miserably. I gave way as gracefully as I could manage to Sam, and slipped back out into the open. I could hear the voices continuing their discussion, muffled and slightly distorted by the shape of the little cave they were crouched in.

"It's like a box. It is, John, it's a stone box. Let me

see…"

A slight scraping noise accompanied this moment of quiet, then, "That's it. It's a kist. Looks like it's made with a partially metamorphosed limestone. It could be native rock – Lismore's famous for its indurated limestone basement rock – that's what gives the island its famous fertility. You can see the joint where the lid fits. It's beautifully made. We can't leave this here. Sam?"

Sam jumped. He'd clearly been completely caught up in the moment and wasn't expecting to hear his own name.

"Get out the record pads and take down my dictation, will you?"

Sam unslung the pack he was wearing and pulled out some site record forms. He chewed the end of his pencil as Niall gave terse instructions about the first few boxes on the form: approximate map reference ("We'll do that in a minute, Sam, let's get this down now."), terrain, inclination of the slope, and a few words describing the surroundings. Then he began to dictate in earnest, and Sam's pencil scurried to keep up.

Niall pulled out a carpenter's tape measure, and he and John moved rapidly around the little building reading out measurements, while Sam sketched a map of the structure and notated it with their data. Eventually Niall's commentary ran down and Sam thankfully put the papers back in his pack. He pulled out a large plastic bag, and Niall and John carefully lowered the box onto it. They swathed it lovingly in layers of plastic, and then the two of them carried it to the waiting car. Sam and I followed along behind. I nudged him with my elbow. "Archaeology still all you want it to be?" I asked.

"Yeah," he replied happily. "Everything's good."

We divided up the sandwiches and shared out milky coffee from the flask, then Sam and I sat on the edge of the tiny bay and let the tide nibble our toes while Niall and John went back to finish their field measurements. I watched Sam, who was staring out to sea, shielding his eyes with one long-fingered hand. His hair was getting long, I realised, and as I had the thought he moved his hand and flicked his hair back behind his ears, in exactly the same way as Niall. I grinned to myself, recognising a sign of hero worship.

Niall had been very generous to offer Sam the chance of an internship on his summer dig. There must have been a lot of students queuing up for the chance, and Sam hadn't even started his degree yet. It was looking more and more as though archaeology was the career he was going to pursue. I couldn't complain. He'd met some great people this year, and it was doing his some good to spend some time with women as well as men. That thought triggered a question and I asked it without thinking. "How does Niall know Annette?"

Sam looked at me sideways, his fringe blowing across his eyes again. He dropped his eyes again immediately, and turned to look back out to sea.

"She's his ex-partner," he said shortly.

"Oh." I wasn't quite sure how to take that. From what little I'd seen Niall and Annette seemed to get on perfectly well, although I don't think it was my imagination that she set people's teeth on edge. Her manner was not exactly charming, but she was undeniably attractive. I wondered how recently the relationship had ended.

"I didn't mean to pry," I said (I did, though).

"No worries," said Sam, trotting out one of his favourite kiwi phrases. "They've known each other for ages. I think they were at school together, and they definitely went to the same uni. I suppose they were childhood sweethearts. But things changed and now they're not together anymore."

"He's still happy to work with her, from the looks of it."

"Annette's the best site recorder on the books. Everybody's happy when they can get her. But she's got this goddess obsession. You have to take her with a pinch of salt."

"I know exactly what you mean."

We arrived back at Port Moluag as dusk was setting in, and the midges were beginning to bite. The new test pit was hidden under a tent, and a cluster of bodies stood around it.

Niall jumped out of the car and ran over there, already beginning to speak as he arrived amongst his team.

"Why is this…?"

He was interrupted by Lisbet, who grabbed his arm and hauled herself out of the trench.

"In there now," she said. "You need to see this." Niall was already jumping down into the tent, leaning under the shelter of the tarpaulin that had been stretched over its open end.

"Oh, you little beauty."

Big John, Sam and I reached the site to be greeted with open smiles and handshakes all round.

"What is it?" I asked.

"Bodies," they said, grinning and hugging one another. Lisbet went on. "At least one, possibly two, fully articulated skeletons. In situ burials. We've found our cemetery."

"Well," said John, "that's going to interfere with the plans for Annaid."

Dinner was delayed while the trench was temporarily protected with plastic sheeting, ready for quick access the next day. Then we all gathered in the hall for beans on toast, gallons of tea and coffee, and a noisy and enthusiastic post-mortem of the day's events, at both sites.

The team wanted Niall and John to tell them what we'd found at Annait. They'd all seen the two men carefully carrying in the block of plastic wrap, which was obviously heavy, and they were desperate to learn what we'd found, but Niall smilingly demurred and asked 'the ladies' (to cries of "chauvinist pig, you only call us ladies when you want something") to tell us what they'd found in the new test pit.

"It was a close call," said Lisbet. "We were just cleaning up the last corner, ready to record and close, as per instructions. Ree was in there. I wasn't even paying that much attention – I was getting the plastic wrap ready to bag and refill the pit. Then Ree lets out this squeak…"

"I shouted," said Ree, elbowing Lisbet.

"Sounded more like a squeak to me," said Lisbet, …ing her back. Ree giggled and they patted each other like a pair of school girls.

"All right, you two, get a grip," said John. Lisbet steadied herself and continued. "She found a toe bone. One teeny little phalange. Of course, that meant we had to extend the pit a bit further. To see if it was associated with anything…"

"And it was," squeaked Ree, jumping up and down.

Lisbet looked at her quellingly and completed the story, "We extended the dig into a full sized trench and kept on digging, all afternoon, and at the end of the day I can confirm we have at least one almost-complete skeleton, probably male, probably adult, and a second skull, some ribs and a long bone. Hopefully we can excavate that fully tomorrow, and then we'll be able to say for sure whether we have our monastic cemetery."

"Hold it," said Niall. "Let's take this one step at a time. Apart from wishful thinking, what makes you think these burials are associated with monastic activity, as opposed to any of the other groups that have occupied Lismore at various times in the last few thousand years?"

"This," said Lisbet, whipping a plastic bag out of her pocket and waving it under his nose.

"Oh, yes, that'll do."

The warm grey stone looked like nothing so much as a small, petrified hot-cross bun. It was the perfect size to fit in one hand, and was smooth and rounded. Even the edges of the incised cross were soft and worn, as if it had been frequently handled.

"A proper prayer stone," breathed Niall. "Well done, girls. Well done all of you. I should go away more often."

"I'm sorry," I said. "What's a prayer stone?"

Everyone turned to look at Niall, but he gestured to Lisbet. "Do the honours?" he requested.

Lisbet handed round the plastic bag so that we could all handle and admire the object within. "A prayer stone is our word for it. Only one has been found before, and we found it last year, at a hermitage on a wee island off the coast of Islay. John wrote it up in last year's dig report.

"It's a small stone, easy to handle, pecked out on one side

with a cross: just like this one, although the stone was darker. We think it might have been used to focus concentration during prayer, rather in the way a modern Catholic uses rosary beads. Rosaries are more complex of course, but the proposed function fits the object. There seems to have been a focus on stone objects during the early monastic period, from huge crosses erected in the landscape to the piles of white pebbles left at places associated with various saints. Remember that dig at Baliscate? They found heaps of white pebbles, almost certainly left by pilgrims."

I nodded, remembering my own visit, unexpectedly livened by the presence of my son and his boss.

"Don't forget the pillow stone," said Ree, nudging Lisbet from behind.

"As if." Lisbet regarded her with mock scorn, then went on with her lecture. "The pillow stone is recorded from a dig on the Shiant Isles, in the Minch between the Outer Hebrides and Skye. Superficially similar to this stone, it was larger than a head, roughly spherical but carefully rounded and flattened, with a cross pecked out on the top. It was found buried upside down inside the remains of a dwelling, and it's proved impossible to date it with any certainty. But the style of carving would fit with the early mediaeval, later than the founding of the monastery here on Lismore but earlier than its end."

"Was it in a church then?" I asked.

"No, that was definitely a house, but the layers of occupation debris on the Shiants are so complex that it's very hard to be sure what it was doing there. Local legend has it that there may been a hermit on the islands at one point, although at other times in history there were several households living there. Anyway, it's another piece of evidence for the widespread habit of carving religious symbols into stone."

"Did they use other materials as well?" asked Sam. "Like wood or stuff that could have rotted away and we're left with only the stone?"

Everyone nodded at this, and I felt proud of Sam. He was

certainly asking sensible questions.

"Very little in the way of wooden religious artefacts has been found from the period," said Niall. "There's no doubt that carved wooden items are known from the tenth century onwards, but not from the early monastic period. It's true that wood and cloth rot, but we're only looking at a period of a thousand to twelve hundred years before the present, and one would expect some wooden objects to survive, especially if they were in common use. In fact, the soil on Lismore contains quite high levels of lime, as it's formed from the alkaline base rocks of the island, and there's a very good chance that if wood or textile has survived in the ground for a thousand years, this will be the place to find it. Maybe tomorrow, eh, ladies?"

The ladies in question failed to respond to the latest evidence of sexism from their glorious leader. They were shuffling and whispering among themselves. Annette pushed through them and confronted Niall with her hands on her hips.

"What we want to know," she demanded in ringing tones, "is what you brought back from Annaid. You didn't take a site recorder with you, so you can't have been doing any excavation. Can you?" This was a reasonable comment, as Annette was the official site recorder and had been busy all day at Achnacroish, recording the unexpected discoveries. But coming from Annette it seemed to take on the flavour of a personal challenge. She tossed her hair back and put her hands in her pockets, managing to make even this simple movement seem both elegant and insolent.

Niall's eyes flashed as he responded to her challenge, though his voice remained quiet and controlled. "We did have a more thorough look than we'd originally planned. We have taken photos, done some basic topographical survey, planned out the visible buildings and other features of the landscape and tomorrow Sam will begin the first stage report. In the process of that preliminary investigation, we discovered something that John and I agreed we could not leave in situ. I've recorded positional information in detail, and Sam has that ready to type up."

He made it sound so rational and organised; I couldn't believe his nerve. This morning Niall and John had been poking about in an unsurveyed building, moving stones and doing damage. I hadn't imagined the excitement in their voices, or the sheepish look on John's face now. Despite his fast talking, Niall knew he'd removed something before it had been fully surveyed and recorded, and by doing so he'd broken his own golden rule. I hoped whatever they'd brought back was sufficiently startling to silence the critics and bear out his decision to remove it.

Annette huffed and a look of scorn crossed her face, momentarily rendering it less than completely beautiful. She opened her mouth, but Ree got in first.

"Are we going to see it?" she begged.

"Tomorrow," said Niall firmly. "Tomorrow we'll take stock of today's discoveries and we'll have a look at what John and I brought back from Annaid. I want good light and a night's sleep before I open up the package."

And with that they had to be content. Surprisingly, there was little complaint from the team as they prepared for the night and broke into smaller groups. The students made a batch of hot chocolate and settled down into a serious discussion about the bones they'd been digging. Sam plugged himself into Niall's laptop and began typing at a frenzied speed, as Annette announced that she and Tim would take a look at Annaid first thing in the morning and she wanted the site notes to take with her. I wandered outside past the one lonely smoker and walked through the dunes down to the bay.

The sea muttered against the pebbles and in the half-light of a summer evening the wavelets glittered as they broke. I closed my eyes and breathed in the smell of the sea and the cool evening air, but a pebble shifted under my feet and I had to open my eyes again while I caught my balance. A tawny owl hooted along the dunes, and the sea breeze crept under my collar, making me shiver. I turned away and went to my tent.

7

Everyone was out of bed early the next morning, and when I made my way into the hall for breakfast I saw that Sam was already back at the computer, typing furiously. I wondered if he'd been to bed at all, but he looked bright-eyed and cheerful so I assumed he must have got some rest. Annette was lurking around his left shoulder, and as soon as he printed off each page she added it to the sheaf of papers she was holding. Various other members of the team bustled in and out, talking non-stop, while Niall stood in the doorway giving instructions.

I ended up taking Annette's rostered duty in the kitchen, preparing mountains of sandwiches, washing fruit and buttering scones, hot from the oven. John joined me, and we slogged our way through the preparation of what seemed enough food for several archaeological dig teams. At last we carried the fruits of our labours out to the waiting masses, and all that food disappeared like magic into backpacks and bags.

Tim took his and Annette's to the little car, where Louise and Amanda were already squashed into the back, and we watched as they drove off down the hill, Tim's hand waving nonchalantly out of the window as they went. I didn't think I was wrong to detect a palpable sense of relaxation once Annette was safely out of the way. Sam perched his bum on the table next to me, clutching a mug of coffee. "Finished just in time," he said. "I thought the screen might go up in flames, the way she was staring at it. Or maybe the back of my neck."

"Is she always so intense?" I asked.

"Yep."

We wandered down to the other end of the hall, where

Niall had brought out his find from yesterday, still securely wrapped in layers of plastic. He laid down a set of tools including a knife, scissors and a large hammer, and pulled on a pair of plastic surgical gloves. Lastly, he settled his headband magnifier over his brows. He pulled down the visor and looked round at us, his eyes magnified to a ridiculous degree, then slid it back up again onto his forehead.

"Are we all here?"

John came out from the kitchen wiping his hands on a tea towel. "Rick, you take notes today. Give Sam's fingers a rest."

Rick obediently sat himself down, pen and recording sheets at the ready, and Niall pulled a minute tape-recorder out of his pocket and started it running.

"Ree and co, can you shuffle left a bit? I want the light from the window. Can everyone see?"

"Get on with it," came an anonymous voice from the back of the pack.

"Quiet," growled John in mock annoyance, but Niall just grinned and picked up the knife. He began to remove the plastic coverings, discarding each into a bin under the table. The closer he came to the object, the more slowly and carefully he worked. So far there had been nothing to see but masses of plastic, but no-one lost interest. The room became quieter as he worked on, and as he removed the final layer I could hear a blackbird singing, and the soft shushing of the breeze in the hedge outside. No-one spoke, but the young archaeologists leaned in closer.

"Ree, pass me that bit of local limestone, will you?" Niall held it up to the light, then placed it next to the stone block he had just unwrapped. "What do you think?" he asked John.

Big John leaned forward and took a close look. "Could well be," he said. "Of course, it's impossible to be sure if it was sourced locally. Lismore's indurated limestone doesn't have any visible identifying features." He looked at me as if to assess my understanding, and I shrugged. I had no idea what he meant.

"When this limestone was first laid down it was in a sedimentary environment, probably the floor of a shallow sea. It would have contained the fossil record of the creatures whose death and decay provided the material of which it was made. Over geological time the rock was buried deep enough to have experienced high pressures and temperatures. This process is called induration, and it produces partly metamorphosed rocks.

"The rocks of Lismore still bear many of the chemical characteristics of limestone (it's quite alkaline, which is why it makes good fertiliser) but it's much harder and no longer carries any evidence of fossils. Chemical analysis and a look at its composition under the microscope may give us a better idea of where it's come from, but we can't confirm its source by its appearance to the naked eye."

Niall glanced up. "Occam's razor says that where there are several possible explanations for the same phenomenon, we should accept the simplest one. We are on Lismore, whose basement rocks are indurated limestone. Here is a block of stone found on Lismore, almost certainly made of indurated limestone. Let's proceed on the basis that it came from here, and not start speculating about more exotic sources."

"Agreed. Is it only a block? Or do you still think it might be a kist."

"It's definitely been worked. You can still see the tool marks. That little building where we found it was made of stone, but the blocks hadn't been dressed as neatly as this. Someone took care over it. And if I do this…carefully…" Niall eased the point of the knife into a horizontal crack about half-way along the block and put some pressure onto it. "I think it will separate."

Niall leaned on the knife blade again and it creaked against the stone. He shifted it along a little and attempted to slide it in again. Gradually he worked his way around the block and it became apparent that the horizontal crack extended all the way around. As he worked the knife into the fourth side a chip came loose in a puff of dust and the whole block shifted slightly. Everyone gasped, and John jumped forward to catch it, but it had only moved a few millimetres. Niall put down the knife and took hold of the top of the block. John steadied its lower half and Niall tensed his arms and shoulders. The block separated instantly and neatly into two parts, and it became clear that it contained a rectangular cavity. Before its contents could come into view, Niall placed the lid carefully back onto the kist and wiped his brow. Quietly he turned to Rick and dictated some notes about the proceedings so far. Rick listened, and wrote, and at last Niall was satisfied

"Okay, boys and girls," he said. "Let's see what we've found."

John steadied the kist again as Niall removed the top and carefully placed it onto a plastic dust-sheet on the table at his side. Everyone leaned on each other's shoulders to get a look inside. A gasp went round. I could see a dusty looking lump of something brownish. It didn't look especially exciting, but it was clear that it meant something to the waiting students. John laughed. "Bit Bram Stoker, don't you think?"

Niall snorted, but it was the turn of the students to look confused.

"You pack of TV and computer-game addicts," John chided them. "Don't any of you read?"

Clearly they didn't, so he explained. "Bram Stoker's *The Jewel of Seven Stars*. The mummy of an Egyptian sorceress is represented by her amputated hand, which crawls about the place causing mayhem. It's a classic."

It was my turn to gasp. (A mummified hand? Are you serious?) John shone a torch into the little pocket of dusty space and Niall pulled the magnifier down over his eyes, still constantly dictating to Rick. Sam crushed in close to me as we all craned to look. Ree dodged around us with her camera, getting shots from every angle. Niall pulled back for a moment so that she could take one directly over the box, then he bent back in and moved the contents gingerly with a pair of tweezers. "Some possible survival of cloth here," he said as he delicately poked the top of the object.

A little dust sifted down and the tweezers emerged with a few fibres of cloth, which went straight into a sealed bag. "Possibly linen. That's the first thing that might give us some dating information. Hmm...metacarpals I would say, good preservation of skin. Ragged appearance at the wrist. This was not detached neatly. Can't tell whether it was pre- or post-mortem. Blackening of the skin surface and some deformation of the bone. Burned? Perhaps partially burned. The fist is clenched. Yes. We have definitely got ourselves a hand."

The murmurs of excitement were growing but I felt slightly queasy and backed away a little. I felt as though I needed some fresh air. As I began to turn away it was Niall's turn to gasp. He inhaled sharply, but turned his head away before breathing out again, fully controlled even in his excitement.

He stopped dictating for a moment and peered closely at the mummified hand. "It's holding something," he said. "Ree, record this please. Then I'm going to slowly turn it over." With the hand rolled over it was possible to see fingernails and even some of the whorls and lines on the fingertips. "The preservation is marvellous," said John. "Niall, you always said we might find skin or cloth here, but we were thinking about the limestone-rich soil preserving burials. This is wonderful."

Niall nodded as he carefully prodded the hand with his tweezers, then gently inserted them between the fingers and pulled out a tiny scrap of something. A spontaneous "Ohh," came from the students and Niall quickly sheltered the find with his other hand, as the combined breath of the gathered bodies fluttered the little thing. A brief hubbub of discussion broke out, but faded again as everyone turned their attention back to the table.

Niall cradled the tiny, blackened scrap in his cupped hands. He bent over it reverently, then tipped it into the palm of his left hand and picked the tweezers again. He touched it gently, prodding a little more firmly as the scrap showed resilience. He shook his head and carefully inserted it into a sample bag. He sealed the bag and held it up again, peering closely at it, then wrote up a label and stuck it onto the bag before storing it in a plastic tub. He pressed the lid down and put the tub aside.

"It looks like burnt parchment," he said. "I could almost make out some kind of marking. I want to believe it's an illustrated letter or a picture, but it's impossible to tell. Maybe we'll learn more when we look at it under a microscope. It's a pity I don't have access to the kind of equipment that forensics investigators use. I bet they could see through the burning and make out what's underneath."

"I think I can help you there," I said.

A few minutes later I was tucked in round the corner of the hall, sheltering from the wind as I tried to get a signal on Niall's mobile phone. Eventually it took, and the phone started to ring, and ring. I was about to hang up when a breathless voice answered: "Hello, Dad's phone."

"Hello, Marise, how's things?"

"Okay, thanks. Um…who is this?"

"It's Cassandra Longmore. Actually, it was you I really wanted to speak to. Do you have a minute?"

"Sure, just about. Dad's changing. He's taking me and Bry out to lunch in five minutes."

At the mention of lunch my stomach rumbled and I glanced down at my watch. Almost two o'clock. No wonder my stomach was complaining; we'd been on the go for hours. It's amazing how the time can slip away on these long Hebridean summer days. The sun seems to stand still in the sky. It doesn't even really get dark till ten or so, and it's easy to forget about mealtimes when you're caught up in something interesting.

"Marise, is it possible for Bry to look at an archaeological sample for us? Does it have to go through official channels or something? Or is it impossible for the police lab to be used for private work?"

"Oh, it depends. They're quite keen these days to take in

outside contracts, although you might have to wait a while if they get an urgent enquiry from the force. But if the lab is quiet, and you're happy to pay the price, they can do private work for you. Do you want me to ask Bry how it works? What have you found?"

"Thanks, Mari. That would be great. It's a tiny piece of parchment that's been burnt, and we want to find out if it has any writing on it. If Bry thinks it's worth a look, then we'll put in a proper request. We'll need to know how much it will cost, though."

"No problem. I'll ask him tonight. Can I call you back tomorrow, Cas?"

"This phone belongs to Niall Webster, the archaeologist who found it. Can you or Bry call him back on this line? He'll have a better idea than me of what they can afford to have done."

"Will do. Any messages for Dad?"

"Tell Henry I love him and I'm going to kidnap him and force him to live on a pretty Scottish island with me."

"Ha." Marise sniggered. Henry has been widowed for more than ten years now, and has absolutely no interest in letting another partner interfere with his carefully plotted rounds of golf and meetings. Besides, the golf course is as close as Henry ever comes to nature, and I couldn't imagine a less likely sight than his slightly paunchy, sharp-suit-clad form wandering the hills and beaches of Mull with me. I made the offer about every six months on average – he'd be disappointed if I stopped doing it. I smiled fondly, thinking of my urban friend. Not only can you not take the city out of the boy, it would be almost impossible to get the boy out of the city.

I wandered back to Niall and gave him his phone. "You should get a call tomorrow," I told him. "A friend of mine, Bryan Desart, works for police forensics down in England. He's going to let us know what he can do, and how to go about applying through the police lab to get the sample looked at privately."

"Brilliant," said Niall, giving me a dazzling smile.

By the time I'd had a bite to eat the students had finished all the food I'd helped prepare and were busy unwrapping their extended test pit. Sam positioned himself to take notes in the absence of Annette, and Ree continued her photographic duties, so it fell to Lisbet to carry on the excavation. Niall volunteered himself for dig and carry, putting aside sample bags of soil for later wet-sieving as he went, as Lisbet began the delicate process of exposing the second skeleton.

I'd had enough of body parts, so decided to go for a walk. I followed the road we'd taken the previous morning, but turned left at the crossroads and soon found myself in the tiny village of Port Moluag. The main street boasted only one shop, a general store and post office, and I stopped to look at a few postcards and maps. I picked up a hand-drawn map of the local area, showing the footpath to the church (cathedral, I reminded myself). When I went to pay for it I noticed some bags of locally made oatmeal cookies. I bought up their whole stock. I was sure the hungry mouths back at the dig would make short work of them.

The walk up to the Cathedral of the Isles was pleasantly unremarkable, but when I got there I found that the remnant of the old building that remained, a pleasant white-washed church, still held an aura of sanctity and peace. I sat down on a bench in the churchyard and let the solitude wash over me. With my eyes closed I could hear the distant baaing of sheep and the harsh croak of a crow as it passed over.

There was a humming in my ears, possibly the product of tension, but when I opened my eyes and looked around I saw that the ancient hawthorn and ivy hedge was covered with bees. I glanced down at my feet and realised every clover patch in the churchyard also had its bee. This would not be the place to walk barefoot.

So far my visit to Lismore had exceeded all expectations. I knew I would remember this peaceful, warm afternoon full of the sonorous presence of bees. I sat on, not so much meditating as dozing, until my head fell forward and I startled awake again. As the sun went down the churchyard had fallen into shadow. The bees had long since headed homeward and I followed them, feeling pleasantly relaxed and ready for whatever lay ahead.

By the time I got back to the hall it was almost dark, and everyone was talking about food. The test-pit team had finished for the day, and Sam and John had concocted a hot meal, mostly out of tins. The students were so ravenous they'd have wolfed down almost anything, but I have to admit it was actually pretty good. Over coffee and handfuls of my oat biscuits we all relaxed and shared a post-mortem of the day.

Rick and Lily had opened up a trench across the proposed vallum. They had confirmed the existence of the ditch, but so far found no dating evidence. The test-pit team had completed excavation of the two skeletons, without finding any further evidence, but the balance of probability suggested that the bodies were two males, one of whom had been found with a prayer stone. There was a slight puzzle over the first body, which had some small bones missing, and the speculation was that it had been re-deposited following decomposition at another site, but the weight of opinion was still that they'd found their early monastic cemetery. John held out his hand for Niall's £10, but Niall demurred. "Two bodies do not a cemetery make."

"Exactly how many bodies do you need?" John demanded.

"One more piece of evidence of any kind that places these burials into the monastic period. Anything will do: a gold cross, a monk's robe, the complete gospel of St Matthew. I'm not fussy."

John huffed, but subsided. "Don't worry," said Niall, tucking the bank note into his back pocket "I'll keep it warm for you."

One of the students leaned forward and stirred up the embers of the fire, then put some more wood on it. In the background I could hear voices and the slam of a car door, and then Tim came over to join us. "Nothing new to report," he told Niall. "Annette's off to find us something to eat. Did you leave us dinner?"

A chorus of "No, no," greeted him and he laughed and headed towards the hall. The conversation slowly began to build up again. "Niall," I said. "What do you think we found at Annaid?"

"Well," he replied, "we can only speculate."

Waves of laughter welled up in the darkness around us. Apparently everyone who has ever worked with Niall recognises this as his signature phrase. He sighed forbearingly and put up with it for a few minutes, then defended himself as they well knew he would.

"All we have is a little bit of burnt stuff, but I'd put money on it being a scrap of parchment, perhaps even vellum, with an illustration or writing on it. If it's contemporary with the monastic development on Lismore, then it's contemporary with our skeletons. Down there we found a mummified hand clutching a scrap of something burnt. Up here we have evidence that our new bodies were Christian. The monastic past of Lismore is already well attested. What do you make of it?"

One of the students spoke out of the darkness: "If that hand came from a monk, then does that make the scrap of parchment a bible?"

"I would love it to be an illustrated page from a missal, bible or other religious manuscript. But it could be a part of the monks' records, or something completely unrelated to the monastery at all."

"Go on, Niall, speculate, just this once. What would you most like it to be?"

Niall leaned back against a rock and stretched out his legs beside the fire. His feet were centimetres from mine. His golden hair shimmered in the firelight, and his half-shadowed face was relaxed.

"There's a famous missing book in the history of Lismore."

We waited as he made himself more comfortable. I stretched out my own legs, but Niall bent his again and sat up straight. "About two hundred years after Columba's death, a monk called Adomnan wrote his hagiography; it's known as the 'Life of Columba'. It wasn't uncommon for saints to have numerous versions of their lives published. It helped to spread the cult of the saint. We happen to know, from brief comments in the annals of the abbey on Iona, that around that time another 'Life' was also circulating: the 'Life of Moluag of Lismore'. No-one has ever seen this book – no copies have survived."

"Why St Moluag?" I asked. "I thought Columba was the top saint in these parts."

"It's true that Columba founded a major monastic lineage, based at Iona, and with influence all over the part of Western Scotland known as Dal Riata and beyond. He was famously well born, of the same family as the Ui Neill kindred of Northern Ireland, who had often been High Kings at Tara, and he could probably be considered to be royal himself. That's no doubt part of the reason he had such influence. But he was by no means the only founder of monasteries in these parts.

"The saint known as Moluag is one of a number of other, less well-known characters. His actual name was something like Lugaid, and the name Moluag is his own name with a Gaelic prefix meaning 'my' or 'my dear'. It's claimed to be a sign of how much his people loved him. He came from the monastery of Bangor, on the east coast of Ireland, and Lismore is only one of many monasteries that he's known to have founded during the latter half of the sixth century. He famously founded one on Tiree, which operated in direct competition with a Columban foundation on the same island. It's also possible that the monastic site at Baliscate near Tobermory was founded by Moluag rather than Columba. It's closer to Lismore than it is to Iona, and it would be nice to think that its monks came from here.

"There's even a legend about Lismore, that both saints were racing to be the first to lay their hand on the soil of Lismore, so as to claim the island for their own lineage. Moluag cut off his own thumb and threw it onto the strand, before Columba's boat could land. It's a variant of a legend that pops up all over Alba, and I don't think we should take it too seriously, but you've got to admit it's a bit creepy, given our find at Annaid."

Murmurs of agreement came from the darkness. Annette emerged from the hall and settled herself among us, producing a wave of shuffling as people made room. Niall took a moment to brief her on the latest discoveries at Achnacroish, before asking her to tell us what she and Tim had found out at Annaid. Annette demurred, saying that the purpose of her visit had not been to make new discoveries, but simply to assist Tim with geophysics and to complete the site survey "that was attempted yesterday." Niall thanked her and waited for the murmur of conversation to die down again before he continued.

"Very little physical evidence of St Moluag remains, although a local family still has guardianship of a blackthorn crozier known as the 'Bachuil Mor', which is said to have been Moluag's staff. It would be fantastic if we could prove we had a scrap of the 'Life of Moluag', found on his own island. That would be the find of the century."

"Hey," I retorted. "I thought my chess pieces were the find of the century."

"Sorry, Cas. If we identified an actual piece of the 'Life of Moluag' your chess pieces would pale into insignificance."

"Besides," said Sam, "they were so last year."

"Indeed." Niall nodded at Sam. "New year, new discovery."

"I'll drink to that," I said, raising my mug, and the others joined me. Amanda leaned forward to put more wood on the fire, and the conversation moved on to other digs, in other places, and to hair-raising tales of the exploits of our students, who loyally refused to believe that their leaders could ever have got up to mischief in their own student days.

Later that evening, crawling into my sleeping bag and gratefully clutching its warmth around me, I thought back over the day. I still can't tell whether Niall is interested in me, or just interested in sharing what he does with anyone who will listen. And for every moment in which I see and respond to his good looks and charm, there's another moment where I find myself mentally stepping back, feeling wary of him. I don't know what it is about him, but something doesn't quite feel right.

I don't think it's my lack of self-confidence. At least, it's not only that. There's something almost non-sexual about Niall, something that stops me responding to him the way I did to Ewan, even before I had any idea that Ewan responded to me. But I can't put my finger on it. I rolled over, banging my hip on a stony bit of ground, and wedged myself into a more-or-less comfortable position, expecting to have a long and restless night, but before I knew it I was asleep.

8

By the time the bus dropped me off at the end of my drive I was exhausted. I slung my bag over my shoulder and began to trudge towards the gate. I'd been up at the crack of dawn to pack, as Niall had decided to get straight over to Tobermory with the package for Bry. Sam came with us, as did Lily who needed to visit the pharmacy and had come armed with a shopping list of medical and sanitary supplies for the rest of the team.

The three of them simply made their goodbyes at the bus stop near the pontoon slipway before heading down Main Street. A brief wait for the bus turned into a couple of hours when the first one broke down, and now I was finally home all I wanted was to put the kettle on for a cup of tea and then sink into my bed.

As I reached out to open the latch I wondered who had parked their brand new Range Rover at the end of the drive. You could get access to the big house across the footbridge at the end of my garden, but it was more usual for vehicles to turn into the drive and park nearer the house. I shrugged – I couldn't summon up enough enthusiasm to care.

As I closed the gate behind me and began to walk towards my front door, a figure stepped out round the side of the house. My heart stopped for a moment, then began to beat quickly, as my body processed the sudden jolt of adrenalin. With an effort of will I forced my face to stay blank, and my voice calm, although it shook slightly as I spoke. "Hello, Drew. I wasn't expecting to see you here."

"I don't see why not. After all, it is my house." (It is not. It is not, you swine, it's mine, my home, but I'm not going to say that, I'm not going to give you the satisfaction of watching me react to you.)

"What can I do for you?"

"You've done quite enough already. What's wrong with you? It's bad enough you ran off and made a fool of yourself pretending you can manage on your own, but what you've done to my son is utterly unacceptable." Drew's perfect skin was blotched red and white and his raised voice, varying from its usual iron control, betrayed an underlying whine.

I wasn't taken aback for long. This behaviour I've seen many times before, and usually it's triggered by some action of mine (or, less often, Sam's) that not only defies the norms prescribed for us by my ex, but threatens some kind of embarrassment or exposure to Drew himself. There was only one thing I could think of that would trigger this kind of outburst, particularly given the distance he'd had to travel to confront me in person.

"I see Sam has told you," I said quietly.

"Told me?" he shouted, beginning to pace up and down on the path. After a few steps, he swung round and marched back towards me. He came a fraction too close for comfort, and I stepped back slightly. Drew has always had the habit of intruding on my personal space. As far as he's concerned he's the only person in the world who has personal space – if he wants to intimidate, he'll stand as close as he likes. At just over six feet tall, he loomed over me, something I used to like. What kind of sea change has to happen in a relationship for 'protected' to turn itself inside out and become 'vulnerable'?

The furious, whining voice ran on, "…trying to turn him into a homosexual. I won't have it. You have completely lost any right you might imagine you have to influence my son. From now onwards you will cease to have any contact with him. I will be instructing my lawyers to take action, and I have a top psychiatrist standing by to examine him once I have got him away from your influence."

"Drew, I'm glad Sam found the courage to tell you that he's gay."

"Don't use that word. You're trying to make it sound

normal. My son is ill, but he isn't homosexual. He's been confused by your ridiculous ideas. I was easy on you. I gave you every chance to have a proper relationship with him. I can see now I should have taken him away as soon as he was weaned. Your influence on him is perfidious. It will cease. Now."

I sighed. Why had I been so afraid of him for so many years? It's all just bluster and bullshit. "Drop it, Drew, I'm not in the mood for a fight. I'm tired and I'd like to get inside. Perhaps your solicitor can write to me again?"

"Bitch." Drew grabbed me by the collar and hauled me towards the house. I fell to my knees and struggled to rise again as he dragged me along. When we reached the porch he swung me around and pushed me against the wall, his thigh pressed into my groin. He clamped one hand around my throat and hissed at me. "You…will…have…no… contact."

I struggled against him, trying to pull his hand away from my throat. Even in the terror of the moment I could feel he had a partial erection. (How predictable you are, Drew. Getting off on torturing your ex-wife.) Drew released his grip on my throat just enough to allow me to signal my capitulation, and waited expectantly.

"Sam's almost an adult now. He'll make his own mind up about contact."

Drew snarled and his eyes went completely blank. He wrapped both hands around my neck and squeezed tighter. As his thumbs dug into my skin I began to black out: my vision slowly disappeared from the outside in, until all I could see was his homicidal glare.

Suddenly, the pressure on my throat released and I collapsed to my knees, coughing in breath after breath as my heart raced, trying to drive the oxygen around all parts of my body at once. My ex-husband knelt on the path in front of me, head down, his arm pulled painfully behind his back. In front of him stood Molly, silent, with every tooth bared. Drew twisted his head sideways, trying to get more distance between himself and those fangs.

Ewan looked back over his shoulder at me. "All right, Cas?"

"Yes. Thanks." My voice was hoarse but I could talk.

"Will you call the police, and I'll keep an eye on this guy?"

"Oh." I was taken aback. "Um…Ewan, I think you remember my ex-husband?"

"I know who he is all right. And it's pretty clear what he is. The question is, do you want to call the police yourself or will Molly and I take him round there?" Molly responded to her name by letting out a low, menacing growl. Drew flinched, and Ewan wrenched his arm a little higher.

"Careful," gasped Drew. "I'll sue you for assault, and believe me I'll take you for everything you've got."

"I wouldn't get too attached to that idea, if I were you," said Ewan. "Seems to me that a man who was caught attempting to murder a woman hasn't got too much to complain about if her rescuer bends his arm a little."

"You have no proof of that."

"Ah, well, that's where you're wrong. Cas, reach into my left jacket pocket."

I did so, and pulled out Ewan's mobile phone. It was switched on to camera mode. I flicked back to the most recent picture: there I was, crushed up against the wall with Drew's hands around my throat. It looked even more brutal than it had felt. I turned the phone round and showed the picture to Drew.

"Do you want to call the police, Cas? If they press charges I'd be happy to act as a witness." Ewan's eyes held mine, concern and anger mingled in his expression.

"No, it's pointless."

He clearly didn't agree, but nodded as he saw the look on my face.

I spoke to the crouched man at my side without looking at him. "Drew, I want you to go away. You don't belong here anymore. If you try to see me again I will go to the police."

"And I'll be keeping a close guard on this pic, in case it's needed in the future." Ewan let go of Drew, who sprawled to his hands and knees. Molly edged past him and went to stand by her master.

Drew pulled himself to his feet and made off towards his car. I gazed at his retreating form: tall, slim, well-dressed, perfectly coiffed. How can something so attractive on the outside be so foul inside? He headed off to the road, tires graunching against the gravel. He didn't close the gate.

I leaned against the wall and sighed. Molly rubbed herself comfortingly against me, and I squatted down and buried my hands in her fur. "Good dog, Molly. Good girl."

Ewan strode back from shutting the gate and looked down at me. He held out one hand and pulled me up. For a moment, I thought he was going to wrap his arms around me. That would have been a comfort, but instead he set me on my feet and let go. I tried not to feel disappointed.

"I sincerely hope that's the last time I have to see him," I said, looking gratefully up at Ewan's face. "Thank you," I added, with sincerity. "It was so lucky you came along at that moment."

"Actually, I've been coming by every day after the last bus goes through, to make sure the place was still locked up tight. Mrs McD's holiday let was broken into the other day, so I figured any empty house might be at risk. Besides, Dad told me to."

"Please thank Hector for me. I don't know what I'd have done if you hadn't been there."

Ewan shuffled restlessly. Obviously I was being too effusive in my thanks. I hauled myself to my feet, biting down on a moment's surge of irritation. Drew had bred that anger, fuelled in me by the sheer relief of survival. I couldn't take my adrenalin imbalance out on Ewan, even if he was being annoyingly obtuse.

"Thank him yourself. You're coming back to us tonight." Ewan had the presence of mind to force a smile onto his face, although it didn't reach his eyes. "Can't leave you here alone after that."

"Oh, no." I felt a wave of exhaustion pass over me. "I

just want to be at home."

Ewan shook his head.

"Please, Ewan, I'll be fine. Drew won't be back. Anyway, I'll lock the doors. I can't cope with any more company tonight. I just want to be alone."

"All right." Ewan whistled to Molly and she came to heel. "I won't tell Dad anything."

"You can tell him I'll be along to see him in a day or two. I will, too. I have a feeling he'll enjoy hearing about Sam's exploits on Lismore."

"I will." And with that he was gone.

9

I fumbled my key out of my purse and opened the door. I dropped my bag on the kitchen floor and went straight round the house, checking the back door and all the windows. Whatever Drew had been doing round the side of the house, there wasn't any sign he'd tried to get in. In the middle of checking I thought I heard a car. I ran back through the kitchen into the back porch, sweat already springing onto my forehead. No Range Rover. It must have been passing traffic. I locked the door and leaned against it, panting, telling myself to be calm. As my heart rate began to slow again the phone rang, making me jump.

"Mum, you'll never guess."

"Sam!" I snapped into mother mode, straightening my back reflexively as I heard the cheerful, enthusiastic syllable issue from my mouth. I've had years of practice at putting on a happy face for my beloved son. Whatever happened between Drew and me, my mantra had always been 'Sam must never know'.

"We've excavated a third body. It was amazing. It had lost its left hand. John says that the bone end shows signs of healing, so the person who lost their hand lived on for a while after the hand was removed. The hand in the box has to belong to it."

"Cool," I said, perking up despite myself.

"Mum, don't say cool. You're too old."

"Hah," I said. "For your information, 'cool' was old when I was your age. It's just come round again. Anyway, does this mean the hand and the kist are definitely to do with the monastery?"

"It must do. Annette is really pissed. She came back from Annaid full of how the site was definitely to do with goddess worship, the cave represents the womb etcetera. She reckoned the hand was some kind of offering, but Niall pointed out that the handless corpse was lying at the same excavation level as the first two skeletons, one of which had a prayer stone. So all the skellies must be related to the monastic period. Annette won't accept it until she sees what's on the wee scrap of parchment we sent away."

"Did you get it away safely, then?"

"Yep. We took it down to the post office in Tobermory. It went recorded, signed for and triple insured. Niall is paranoid it's going to get lost in the post."

I laughed. It was lovely to hear Sam enjoying himself, and that reminded me that even under present circumstances I couldn't completely regret my marriage to Drew. Without him I would never have had Sam. I hung up and went back to the kitchen to boil the kettle for tea. There was no power.

Typical. Bloody typical. Along comes a random power cut just when the only thing standing between me and a good night's sleep is a mug of tea and a warm bath. Sulking, I poured myself a glass of water and made my way into the living room, where my mattress and bedding were still piled up in a corner awaiting the repairs to my leaking roof. I manipulated them into roughly bed-like order, kicked off my shoes and sat myself down.

Suddenly the whole situation got on top of me and tears squirted from my eyes, dripping down my nose and blurring my vision. Once I started I couldn't stop, and cried on and on until my breath caught in my aching throat, and my sinuses throbbed. My head felt as though it had been squeezed in a vice, and the more I cried the more it hurt, making me cry even more at the sheer misery of it all.

I crawled under the covers and lay curled around myself. More bitter tears scalded my eyes as I looked back over my life. "All I wanted was to be loved," I wailed into my pillow. "I didn't deserve this life. How could this have happened to me?"

I thought back to my own adolescence: that time of innocence and ignorant, blissful expectation, taken away from me in an instant on the night of my wedding. A naive teenager, kept away from the realities of sex and boys, allowed to fall prey to an older, experienced man, who valued me only for my looks, my trophy status. How could my grandparents have let that happen to me? Why hadn't they protected me?

I wallowed in self-pity, but I couldn't keep it up. Inevitably, thinking about my teenage self took me back in memory to the real experiences of that life, and I found myself reliving the events that had led up to my marriage: my first meeting with Drew at the New Year's Dance, and my immediate feelings of attraction and liking for the good-looking, well-mannered and undeniably wealthy man.

He had seemed so much older and more experienced than me, though in reality he'd barely finished his business degree. Still, from the point of view of a seventeen-year-old, twenty three looked like real maturity. We soon found a quiet corner away from the crowd, in which to dance and talk in relative privacy, and I felt safe from parental interference since Granddad was in the pub and I didn't expect to see him before twelve.

But Granddad had emerged unexpectedly and bullied me home early, waylaying me as I made my slightly unsteady way to the Ladies'. I'd been furious; how dare he ruin my wonderful evening on the flimsy excuse that he felt ill and wanted to go home?

Later it dawned on me that he must have seen me dancing and drinking in the dark with Drew. The spot we had chosen was overlooked by one of the windows of the pub. Even then, I didn't register that his concern had not been for my obvious flirting with Drew, but rather with the look that he had seen on the man's face, illuminated by the light from the village hall. He didn't tell me that until much, much later. Much too late.

Granddad had kept to himself his fears, his doubts (to be fair, his full and correct understanding of Drew, from the very beginning). Instead, he tried to make me understand that I was too young; that I needed to go out into the world and study, work, live life for a while, before making a decision of this magnitude. His advice fell on deaf ears. By the time he spoke to me, I was already making plans to creep out of my bedroom window at night for a secret rendezvous, and by March Granddad had given in and we set the date for the wedding.

Another realisation that didn't come to me until much later was that Drew must have fallen hard himself, to ask me to marry him when I refused to sleep with him unwed. Looking back, I'm frankly surprised he bothered, but in those first few months he wooed me like a princess, and I was won over completely by his charming exterior, his gifts, and the promise he held out of a lifestyle where there could be no want that was not immediately satisfied. By the time I understood it was Drew's wants that were to be satisfied, and discovered the penalties for not performing as required, with grace and decorum, it was too late. I had sold myself into genteel slavery, and my own sense of shame prevented me from admitting it, even to myself.

Why did I not see through him? Perhaps that was asking too much. My head had been turned by the money and the lifestyle Drew stood for, but he wouldn't have got far if I hadn't also been powerfully in lust with him. I tried to recall how much I knew about sex before I met Drew. Of course I knew the mechanics – no-one can grow up on a farm and be ignorant of the facts of life – and I suppose I had some grasp of the driving power of sex. Human beings were animals, after all, and I'd dealt often enough with the rams brought in to tup the ewes, or with the boar in his quiet paddock, who sometimes took it upon himself to go on a pen-wrecking rampage if he wasn't let in to the sows when he thought he ought to be.

I remember hiding in the loft and spying on the stallion which was brought in to service one of Granddad's two young mares. That had been a great palaver, and a lot of fuss made over a beast that when all was said and done didn't seem to have *done* very much. There was no denying the mare's eagerness for her suitor, though. The sound of her welcome, and the stallion's ringing demands, had filled the stable yard.

I could almost feel the prickly straw poking through my shorts, and smell the summer fragrance of hay, which lingered in the loft even to the end of winter and always made me feel warm and sunny, whatever the temperature outside. As I basked in the memory, it brought to mind another farm animal of far more immediate interest to a lonely adolescent. Every year Granddad took on one or two farmhands from the local towns, and of course the shearing gangs came in late spring, with their cooks and rousties, often girls whom I'd befriend for a week or two, before they all moved on to the next farm.

In the summer of the year I turned sixteen, Granddad hired a man to work the whole season. He arrived with Granddad in the ute, after a visit to town, and Granddad told us no more than "This here's Cam Cameron. He'll be staying till the hay is in." Cam took up residence in the outbuilding attached to the barn, which had once been an office and was now disused. He was nice enough, if a little quiet: calm, solid, good-looking but non-threatening. The human equivalent of a Welsh pony, I thought to myself.

Granddad worked him like a horse in harness, which is to say as hard as he worked himself. I eyed Cam from a distance all summer, taking in his brown, broad back as he worked in the kitchen garden for Nanna, or spying on him from afar as he moved the sheep to new grazing. He was willing but not altogether at home on the farm, and I wondered what his story was. It wasn't like Granddad to take in waifs and strays, but Cam had an undeniable air of gratitude towards the man who had employed him.

He fascinated me, and I took to ambushing him as he made his way home from the outer paddocks, or hiding in the branches of the old pine tree by the back of the barn, so as to ask him questions unexpectedly, out of thin air. I got nothing out of him but that he came from Wellington ("city boy," I said, scornfully) and that he had grown up on his uncle's farm ("so there," said his look, although he didn't deign to vocalise it). So: not a city boy, then. Or maybe only one in comparison to the local boys, many of whom thought a town of fifty houses was a big place.

I couldn't say when I first realised that he watched me as much as I watched him. He was much more subtle about it, but at last I began to notice. I didn't have the sense to understand that I was playing with fire. I only saw that it was my prerogative to watch and study him. How dare he attempt the same with me? I determined to have it out with him.

One morning I got up in the half-light before dawn and crawled out of my window, in jeans and T-shirt but without bothering about my boots. I crept silently over to the barn, and listened. There was no sound from the old office, but I could hear a noise of water splashing inside the barn. I went to the door and looked. In the corner by the old sink, Cam was washing himself. He was naked. His strong, sturdy body was brown from head to toe, with only a slight sun-darkening of the skin of his forearms and the back of his neck. I could see the play of muscle as he lifted one leg to dry it, and a twist in the thigh muscle that told of an interesting scar. I was frozen to the spot.

Unable to take my eyes off him, I watched him finish drying himself and turn to reach for his jeans. As he pulled them on I must have made a sound, because he suddenly looked up and saw me. My face couldn't redden with embarrassment; I already felt fever-hot all over.

Cam stood and looked at me stolidly. His expression didn't change, but he gestured at me to come in, and bowed slightly, mockingly, as I stepped across the floor towards him. A smile flickered across his face, then faded as I approached him and my eyes were caught and held by his. They were brown like mine and flecked with green that reflected the early sun entering the small, high window at the head of the barn.

I stood directly in front of him. I couldn't look away, and my eyes held him too. He made no movement, but stood as still as a well-schooled pony until I stopped millimetres away from him. I looked down at the half-bare body immediately in front of me, and then back up at his face. Cam made no sound, but he swayed slightly and the full length of his body came into contact with mine. One foot stepped back slightly as I lost balance, but then I steadied myself and leaned into him. Still with our gazes locked on one another, we stood almost motionless, perhaps trembling a little. I know I was.

I felt my lips part, but couldn't think of anything to say. Cam's cool breath played across my brow and I shivered. I felt a great wave of feeling pass through me; I couldn't tell if it was desire, or fear. All of a sudden I wished I was anywhere else but here, but I felt the inevitability of whatever was to happen next. I'd passed beyond the bounds of safety, and the imminence of danger thrilled along my nerve endings.

As my knees began to sag under the weight of my own emotional turmoil, a slight sound caught my attention. Outside the barn a faint whistling could be heard, an almost recognisable tune, and with it the scuff of worn boots on the paving stones outside the house.

"Granddad," I breathed. With that I swayed backwards, and Cam caught at my arm as I lost balance. He set me back onto my feet, then turned away and finished dressing. I climbed straight into the loft and lay flat, smelling the fragrance of the new summer's hay as I listened to Granddad enter the barn and give his instructions for the day. Cam had only stayed a few more days, and I hadn't been at home when he left. I've never been able to decide if I was sorry Granddad had come along when he did. I'll always wonder what might have happened. And how lucky it was that we'd heard him coming.

I shuffled about in my soggy bed of misery, then sat up and stared into the darkness. I suddenly understood there was no luck involved. How often had I heard Granddad whistle a tune? Sure, he whistled to the dogs, and when he was deep in concentration he would hum a tuneless drone – Nanna would hit him with a knitting needle and tell him not to annoy her with the silly sound – but it was rare for him to whistle a melody. . That day we didn't hear his footsteps until after I'd recognised the whistle, and by the time I did he was almost at the barn door.

He must have known I was in there with Cam. He gave me the chance to escape without getting into trouble. As I thought about that, I began to realise something else: Granddad hadn't been saving me from getting into trouble with him. He had recognised that I might have got out of my depth, and provided the opportunity for me to make a graceful escape.

"Thanks, Granddad," I whispered in the dark, and the tears threatened to fall again. This time I wasn't pitying myself, but crying for the man who had raised me, when there had been no mother or father to take care of me; who had let me make my own mistakes while trying always to be there if I took a step too far. With Drew I had gone where he couldn't help me. I had done it to myself, and no one but me can take responsibility for that.

10

When I woke the next morning the clouds had lifted, metaphorically and in reality. I felt as though the tears (and the whole wretched confrontation with Drew) had washed away the cobwebs from my mind and left it clear. I was finally free of him. Sure, he'd frightened me with his bullying tactics, but not at any moment during yesterday's events had I felt tempted to give in to him. Those days are over.

The sun pouring in through the windows enhanced the brightness of my outlook. Towering cumulus clouds with ragged edges promised a day of sunshine and showers. I pulled on a high-necked blouse to hide the bruises that were coming out on my neck, the marks of fingers and thumbs clear for all to see. I unpacked the case I'd been using on Lismore and shoved the dirty clothes into the laundry basket.

Pulling out a damp towel jogged my memory and I laid it down and carefully unrolled it. The Calgary Queen tumbled out onto the bedclothes and lay looking up at me. I carried her downstairs and stood her on my desk. Was it my imagination, or did she look pleased to be home?

The power was back on and the milk was still okay for tea, but the freezer had defrosted and the bread in its bottom drawer was soggy and unappetising. I cleared the freezer drawers and threw the lot away. That settled my plans; I would have to go to Tobermory for emergency supplies. I decided to get the car out of the garage and make a day of it. Who knows, I may have to sell the car if my finances don't improve. It really is one luxury I can't afford, so while I still have it, I might as well make the best use of it I can.

I made up a thermos of tea and threw a packet of biscuits

and a slightly wrinkled apple onto the front passenger seat. At the last minute I nipped back in to use the phone. Bernie wasn't home. Closing the gate behind me I turned not left, towards Dervaig and Tobermory, but right onto the Calgary road, on the first stretch of a long day. Going the long way round it would take me all morning to get to Tobermory, but it must be the best part of two years since I last drove down the west coast of Mull. I was looking forward to it.

As I drove I kept the wipers on intermittent. Brief showers pocked the windscreen and then passed, interspersed with glorious bursts of sunshine. Between the rain flurries it was hot in the car and I kept rolling down the window, then having to put it up again when the next shower fell. Somehow I felt as confused as the weather. The burst of energy that had woken me had worn off and I felt enervated. The single-track road demanded focus and my attention kept wavering as my mind flickered randomly from one thought to another.

Suddenly I rocked in my seat as the car jounced through a pothole, and I took a firmer grip on the steering wheel and my concentration. There was a formless ache behind my eyes, not quite a headache but a bleary-eyed and woolly-headed warning that one might be on its way. I suffer migraines rarely, but when they hit they are debilitating. I considered turning back, but instead gritted my teeth and told myself not to be so pathetic.

When I came abreast of the little public toilet building at Calgary Bay, I swung the car sharply right into the parking space and turned off the engine. A sudden pain had gripped me and I hunched forward, holding my abdomen. After a moment the discomfort eased and I straightened up, only to double over against another griping cramp. I got out of the car and ran across the road into the toilet building, but ten minutes of contemplation produced no results beyond a dull, heavy ache in my belly. As I ducked out of the doorway and crossed the road again the skies opened.

I jumped into the car just in time to avoid a complete soaking. The view out of the car's windows was completely obscured by cascades of water sheeting down the glass, its greyness relieved for a moment by a flicker of lightning. Somehow the grey torrent drumming on the roof above my head released a barrier in me and tears poured from my eyes.

I stared sightlessly through the double curtain of tears and rain, shaking my head as the endless, painful sobs shook my body. I cried a river, hardly pausing to breath between one sob and the next. As quickly as it had started, the rain stopped and watery sunlight filled the car. I sniffed loudly and cleared my throat, wincing as the pain reminded me of last night's events.

No wonder I was out of sorts. Of course, Drew had attacked me physically before, but usually he was careful to keep his hands clean. Over all the years of emotional misery with him, he had rarely left visible bruises. Reliving the experience, I realised that I did feel frightened of him, but that emotion was vastly outweighed by the embarrassment and shame that filled me when I reflected on the fact that Ewan had witnessed the assault.

I saw again the blankness of Drew's eyes as he gave into rage and attempted to throttle me. If Ewan hadn't come along at exactly the right moment I'd probably be dead. Of course, Drew would have been sorry afterwards. He always is, even while he's excusing himself by saying that I made him react that way. Or course it was my fault. I provoked him.

I shivered in revulsion, remembering how he would manipulate me into blaming myself for his behaviour. I wonder who he has found to bully now that I'm no longer around. Perhaps he hasn't found anyone. All that pent up anger and hatred, with no readily available victim on whom to expend it.

That might explain why he reacted so badly last night. He would never allow himself to behave that way in front of his colleagues, and you can't do it to the domestic staff – they tend to leave. In Drew's world that's one of the roles of the wife: to be the verbal punching bag that allows him to vent his emotions without fear of reprisal.

I guess he comes by it honestly. I only met Drew's father a few times before he died, but he spoke to me with a kind of distant contempt, as if I was so far beneath him that he couldn't really see me. He frightened me, and he wasn't much more pleasant with his son.

Drew spent his life trying to get his father's approval, and the closest he ever came was the occasional grudging acknowledgement that he had performed adequately. Perhaps Longmore Senior saw praise and enthusiasm as signs of weakness, but his contempt bred weakness in Drew, who thinks that the way to appear strong is to beat down anyone who can potentially be made subordinate, while fawning over those he sees as superior. It seems to work in business – at least, Drew's companies and investments generally do well – but it makes for a difficult home life.

If there's one thing I've tried to give Sam, it's a kind of open-hearted self-confidence that is not threatened by the success of other people. Watching him at work in Niall's team was reassuring: he seemed at ease with all the members of the team, with the possible exception of Annette. And school seems to have been good for Sam. Not enough exposure to female role models, but plenty of good male ones, perhaps including, although I admitted it reluctantly, the boy who had taken Sam's virginity, introduced him to adult relationships and enabled him to accept that he was gay.

I still felt a shiver of distress as I thought of Sam being inducted into his first sexual relationship at the age of fifteen, and if Magnus had been standing in front of me I would have had a bundle of pithy remarks to throw at him, but Sam didn't appear to have taken any long term harm from the experience. Even though it was my beloved only son who had been seduced, I had to accept Sam had got off lightly. I knew from my own experience that his first time could have been much, much worse.

The car windows had all steamed up and I turned on the engine to start the fan and clear the condensation before pulling away. As I turned the key I glanced reflexively at the petrol gauge. I turned the engine off and on again, refusing to believe what I saw. The arrow indicated that I had less than an eighth of a tank of petrol. Surely I'd filled the tank the last time I drove to Tobermory? I cast my mind back but couldn't remember. Never mind, the evidence was right in front of me. Not only did I not have enough petrol for the coastal jaunt I'd planned, I'd be lucky to make it to the nearest petrol pump, in Tobermory, without running dry en route.

I put my head down on the steering wheel and laughed – a panicky, slightly out-of-control laugh akin to the tears I'd so recently shed. Imagine if I'd run out of petrol halfway down the west coast of Mull, with no mobile phone signal and miles from the nearest house.

I wiped my eyes again and reversed the car, turning towards home and onwards to Tobermory. I felt light with a combination of regret and relief. At least the car was now pointed in the right direction, but I wasn't so sure about myself. What am I going to do about my house, and my life? What am I going to do about Drew? What else is going to go wrong? I had an unpleasant suspicion that there was more to come.

11

The journey back was much calmer. That ferocious downpour had seen off the rain for the time being, and the whole landscape remained bathed in sunshine. When I passed home the petrol gauge had hardly dropped, and I climbed the Dervaig hairpins before the petrol warning light came on. I watched the dial with one eye as I made my way along the side of the Mishnish Lochs. The engine didn't miss a beat but, even so, I coasted down the steep hill into Tobermory on the fumes. As I rounded the corner and aimed towards the garage, I realised the tanker was in delivering fuel and the pumps were all closed.

I parked the car by the waterfront and planted myself in a cafe to wait, nursing a double cappuccino and a large piece of lemon cake and justifying my purchase with thoughts of all the petrol money I'd saved by not driving round the island. I pulled out my mobile phone and turned it on to check whether I should add some more credit while I was near the bank.

There were two missed calls from Niall. Maybe he'd already got word back from Bry about the mysterious scrap, although it seemed a bit soon. Even though Niall had sent it away immediately, there could hardly have been enough time for it to be delivered, let alone undergo a proper scientific analysis. Maybe they'd found something else at the dig on Lismore.

I returned the second call but the signal went straight to voice mail. I left a message to say I'd called, and that I'd phone again. By that time the last drops of coffee were cold and the petrol tanker had swung itself round the corner and up the hill, on its way back to the ferry. I shrugged my coat on and strolled out of the cafe, stopping to allow the local bus to pass by before crossing the road back to my car. With a squeal the bus braked sharply and stopped right in front of me. A figure darted round the front of the bus and grabbed me by the arm. It was Niall.

"Is Sam with you?" he asked.

I looked at him in confusion. "I thought Sam was working with you on Lismore?"

"He is. He was." Niall could hardly speak. "His father came. In a helicopter. He took Sam away. He had a gun."

I stared at Niall, willing the words to make sense.

"A gun?"

"Sam's father came to the dig site. The chopper landed in the fallow field and Mr Longmore came running out of it. Of course, we didn't know who he was, but Sam knew, before it even landed. His Dad took him by the arm and tried to drag him to the helicopter. Sam struggled, and then his Dad pulled out a pistol and started waving it about. He said if Sam didn't go with him he'd shoot him – he'd rather have a dead son than a queer one and he was going to fix that problem one way or the other. Sam yelled at Lily to grab his wallet and phone from his tent, and then he went off with his Dad. That was yesterday. We haven't heard anything since. Have you heard from him?"

"No, not a word."

"I think we should go to the police."

I stared at Niall. My mind was spinning. What on earth was Drew playing at?

"He's been missing for 24 hours now, and he was abducted at gun point. I think we should get the police involved."

"No, no." I was still struggling with the implications of Niall's account. "Drew would never hurt Sam." I willed myself to be calm and looked Niall straight in the eye. "I'm afraid this behaviour is not altogether surprising. Drew doesn't like his world vision to be challenged. He probably believes he can change Sam's mind. He certainly already thinks Sam's sexuality is my fault. But he loves Sam. I'm sure he won't harm him."

"I can't go back to the dig as if nothing has happened." Niall's wide-eyed look faded as he calmed himself. "Anyway, I had to hitch a lift with the Tobermory RIB service, and now they're out on another job. I'll find somewhere to stay in Tobermory. Will you let me know if you hear anything? And I'll do the same for you, if Sam contacts me."

"I thought you had your own boat? I mean, at the excavation."

"It's out of the water. Something wrong with the fuel feed. John has it in bits on the shingle. I thought Sam might end up with you, so I left you messages. I thought if you didn't reply I would get the bus or a taxi over the hill to see if Sam was at your house. I was trying to stop the bus when I saw you."

My breathing had settled, and Niall was calmer too, although I wasn't entirely convinced he wouldn't contact the police as soon as I left him. There was no point in that. Drew has thrown Daddy paddies before, when things haven't gone his way. Conciliatory parenting isn't his style – it's his way or no way – but I'm sure Sam will have calmed him down by now, and we'll hear from him at any moment.

"Why don't you come back with me to Dervaig?" I put on my most persuasive face. "That way if Sam contacts either of us, we'll both know, and I can run you back into Tobermory tomorrow morning if you want to catch that boat."

"That's kind of you, Cas, but I don't want to be out of mobile phone range. Unless you've planted a phone mast in your garden since I last visited?"

"Oh." I'd forgotten the signal problem. "Of course. I understand. I'll leave you to it then." I turned to walk away from Niall, then spun back: "You will call me as soon as you hear?"

"Of course I will, as soon as I hear anything at all. But Cas, why don't you stay? I can book a couple of rooms in Tobermory, and that way we'll both be in range if Sam tries to call."

"No, I couldn't…"

"Yes, you can. It's the least I can do."

"Niall, that's really kind of you. And if Sam does call and needs us we will be able to respond quickly."

He nodded. "Do you have your car with you?"

"Yes, it's parked over the road." I stood still for a moment, trying to get my head round the latest twist in the day.

Niall took my hand and dragged me through the doors of the nearest hotel, where he booked the last two available rooms, opposite one another on the first floor. I nipped into the Co-op for a toothbrush and a pack of spare underwear, while Niall borrowed my keys and filled the car with petrol. I walked back down the waterfront towards the car, taking the chance to look the man over as he stood in profile, staring out across the bay.

He was wearing his usual shabby chic: comfortable, khaki trousers and jersey that looked effortlessly casual and probably cost several of my arms and legs. On his head was the Tilley hat I'd seen him wearing the day we met him at the ferry; the day, last summer, when we'd walked Calgary Bay up and down in search of the Calgary Chess Queen, and started the seeds of a workable friendship.

I think we function well as a team, hardly needing to exchange a word, but getting tasks done as quietly and efficiently as possible. Such a contrast to Drew's crisis response, which is to stand in one place and bellow until someone fixes the problem (someone always does).

I looked Niall over again, surreptitiously, as I dumped my shopping bags in the boot and pulled out the bits I would need tonight. He's gorgeous, and nice, and clearly concerned about my son. He must be a really good leader if he cares this much about all his team members. I like him very much, and he'd make a great partner. He has a ready-made shared interest with Sam, and after all there isn't too great a leap between mentor and father-figure. I could see that Niall was attractive: little things, like the endearing way he pushes his fringe out of his eyes, catch my eye and I see how good looking a man he is.

So why do I not respond? More to the point, he's single, attractive and employed. He should be surrounded by potential girlfriends, and yet the only one I know about is Annette, whose general air of thinly veiled hostility seems to indicate that whatever she may have once felt for Niall is dead and buried, although it was clear she must still feel something for him, good or bad, given her touchy behaviour on the dig site.

I fretted over Sam all afternoon, at first alone in my room, looking out the window and wondering where on earth Drew had taken our son, then later as we ate (but hardly tasted) a meal in the little restaurant, and settled into the guests' lounge to sit out the evening. I wondered whether I should contact my solicitor and ask her advice, but there was nothing I could do until her office opened the next morning. My eyes ached with unshed tears and my throat throbbed in sympathy. I hoped I was right in saying that Drew would never harm Sam. Until yesterday, I hadn't thought he would ever go so far with me.

Niall was restless, and kept pacing the floor. I was staring at the television, although I have no idea what programmes were on. I paid attention when the news came on, watching it as if the big news in my life was somehow going to be answered by the calm tones of the newsreader. A bulletin from the Middle East, a politician's speech, some football – none of it was any good to me. "Cas?" Niall was standing in front of me, in the way of the weather forecast. "I'm going to stretch my legs before I turn it. Would you like to join me?"

"Good idea." I jumped up and grabbed my coat. The opened door revealed that a haar had blown in off the sea and concealed all details of the town. There was a feeling of silence in the misty street, even though I could clearly hear the bass thump of music from the pub next door. As I stepped over the threshold of the hotel, the fog-horn suddenly sounded, and I jumped and tripped. Niall caught me as I was about to fall face-first into the road, and I grabbed onto his upper arm and held on while I found my balance.

As I straightened up, Niall's arm went round my waist, the pub door opened and Ewan walked out. His eyes flicked from mine to Niall's and back again. I flinched mentally and broke eye contact. Ewan nodded and grunted, then turned and went back into the bar. The mist eddied a little in the wake of the draught he left behind. For heaven's sake, can life get any more complicated?

We walked the length of Main Street and back again, both of us with our heads down, watching our footing. Somehow, the swirls of mist made it harder to keep our footing, and more than once I swayed and caught at Niall's arm again. He tripped on the old paving stone outside the Post Office, the one that sticks up a bit. We must have looked like a pair of drunks reeling down the street. A couple of cars passed us, engines sounding muffled and headlights creating opaque yellow patches in the fog. When we got back to the pub the music seemed quieter, although it might just have been that the fog had grown thicker.

The fog-horn moaned its regular, mournful cry, warning ships away from the lighthouse out at the point. For a moment I felt disoriented, as if this was no longer the same familiar town, but the breeze shifted and swirled the fog around our faces and I smelled the pungent reek of seaweed and a distinct whiff of yeast: the brewery must be going through its cleaning cycle, venting the dirty water from the vats into the burn.

"That's Tobermory's smell all right," I muttered as we fell back into the doorway of the hotel. Niall checked his phone, now we had some light to see by. No messages. My phone, the same. We stood in the empty lounge and looked at each other. "I'm going to try and sleep," said Niall at last, "in case we get a call in the night."

I nodded wearily and set off upstairs behind him. I hardly remember the last time I stayed in a hotel with a man, although it would definitely have been Drew. With him I would have been constantly worrying about my looks and decorum, not wanting to let him down or to do anything to give him an excuse to be angry. I could see myself, slight and pale in a red dress, fixing my make-up in the mirror and planning how I would walk, stand, the timbre and tone of my voice; everything controlled as rigidly as possible, in order to reduce the likelihood of meeting with disapproval.

Even so, I would have been hoping that a meal, perhaps a show, a night away from home might result in some communication between us, some sign that there was still life in our marriage. Forlorn hope. And now here I am with a completely different kind of man, and yet the situation is equally lacking in romance.

I tossed my phone and purse down on one of the twin beds and fell on top of the other. I lay on my back and stared at the ceiling, listening to the fog-horn crying like a lost creature in the night. I amused myself trying to imagine what sort of a beast would make such a noise, but the image that sprang immediately to mind was Sam at seven, standing before me with his hands clasped behind his back, reciting Lewis Carroll's *Jabberwocky*, word perfect. "All mimsy were the borogroves," I murmured to myself. What sort of beast had taken my son away? (The jaws that bite. The claws that snatch. Indeed.)

I thought of Sam as he is now, standing before his father with the same steady look. Sam the Steadfast. Sam the Brave. Telling his father he was gay, knowing already that it wasn't going to go well. I know my imaginary picture is wrong – Sam must have told his Dad over the phone, almost certainly from the dig site on Lismore. What triggered his decision to tell Drew now? How had Sam handled that situation? I hadn't yet had the chance to find out, though I'd seen Drew's reaction for myself, only yesterday. Drew must have gone straight from his confrontation with me to Lismore, to collect Sam. Straight from assaulting me to taking his son. My son. Where was he?

"What are you up to, Drew?" My voice was croaky, tears pressing behind my eyes but unable to fall. I fingered the bruises at my throat, swallowing past the lump there. No use to cry now. No use at all. I would ask Sam the next time I saw him. He would tell me everything. I would comfort and protect him, and if necessary I would use Ewan's photo to blackmail Drew.

I saw myself darting in front of the vulnerable figure of my son, holding up the photograph of my ex-husband strangling me at my own front door. Holding it up in front of the monster which suddenly reared up, taller than the hills and crashed down on me with a reek of brine and whisky. I shuddered and woke, with a foul taste in my mouth, to find that it was morning and the fog was still swirling around the window.

My phone was dead. Leaving it switched on all night had run down the battery. I'm not very good at remembering to charge it. I might as well have gone home to Dervaig for all the good it's done me to stay here. I turned off the phone to see if a rest would restore any function, and stood under a cold shower for as long as I could bear it, trying to clear the cloudy feeling in my head.

I had no appetite for breakfast, but forced down some porridge and a mug of tea. Niall managed a full Scottish breakfast and coffee. Clearly he wasn't as worried as I was. Well, why should he be? I appreciated his concern for the youngest member of his dig team, and I suppose that as he had invited Sam to join the Lismore excavation team Niall felt responsible for his welfare, but I couldn't expect him to care in the way that I did. The way only a mother can.

Ten o'clock came and went; we vacated the hotel and still there was no word. Niall went to buy a paper and discovered he couldn't: there'd been no ferry today. Apparently, the fog was so bad in the Sound of Mull that Calmac weren't going to allow the boat to run until it cleared. In Tobermory the mist was thinning, and as the morning wore on the sun began to break through the cloud. We sat in the hotel lounge and I nursed a coffee for as long as possible, but finally couldn't sit still any longer.

"Are you sure you haven't had a message?"

Niall lifted his eyes from yesterday's business pages, which he had apparently been reading word for word. "Nothing," he said bleakly. "I'm going to try phoning again." He took the phone out of his pocket and nearly dropped it, as it vibrated in his hand and the tinny notes of Flower of Scotland began to sound. Niall held the phone to his ear. He seemed to have stopped breathing. I waited, holding my own, willing it to be....hoping for it to be...

"Okay, I'm on my way." Niall put the phone back in his pocket and sprang out of his seat. "It's Sam," he said. "He's on the ferry in Oban. They're on board, delayed but hoping to get the word to head off any minute."

"Is he still there?" (Stupid question, Cas. He's already put the phone in his pocket. Why did Sam call Niall? Idiot, your phone is switched off – no battery, remember.) I pulled my phone out and turned it on again. It showed signs of life, but I had no missed calls or messages. Niall headed out the door and I trotted along in his wake. He still had my car keys in his pocket (how had I failed to notice that?) and headed straight for the car park.

"I'll drive," I called after him.

Niall unlocked the passenger door, then tossed the keys over the car to me. "Take it easy," he said. "We should have plenty of time."

12

I pulled straight into the ferry car park, keeping right to avoid the long line of cars hoping to get a stand-by place on the next run to Oban. The ferry was in, disgorging a slow trail of cars, buses and delivery lorries. Niall was out of the car before I turned off the engine, running towards a tall figure standing by the window of the Tourist Information Centre.

Sam stepped forward and met him in the middle of the road, throwing himself into Niall's arms. The two of them stood, arms wrapped around each other, heads turned together, holding each other so tightly that the wind off the sea blew the golden hair and the dark together, like the plumage of a single, new creature. Not one word had been exchanged.

I dragged in a lungful of air, and realised I'd been holding my breath as a shocking realisation washed over me. My head filled with images of the last few weeks: Sam leaning close over Niall's shoulder to look at a map; Sam and Niall giggling amongst the trees at the Baliscate dig site; Annette's prickly, condescending teasing of Sam, and Sam's strange reserve as he told me Annette was Niall's ex-partner. My own confused attraction toward Niall, whose responses were intermittently friendly but didn't quite make sense to my profoundly heterosexual brain. It all rearranged itself in my mind and the truth became obvious.

Sam and Niall were in love with each other: at this moment so rapt in one another as to be oblivious of all else, including the traffic which had to detour round them. A farm vehicle with trailer passed them, honking loudly, and the boys relaxed their death grip on each other. Niall and Sam left the road and walked towards me, still arm in arm, identical grins of relief on both faces. I plastered something similar on my own and reached out to hug Sam. For a moment we were a unit of three, until Niall withdrew slightly and gave me my moment with my son.

Gave me. I tried not to resent his tact.

I hugged Sam tightly, then held him at arm's length to look him over. "What did he do to you?" I demanded. (So much for taking things slowly.)

"Nothing," Sam said, coming forward and hugging me again, then patting me on the shoulder in a comforting but definitely patronising way. "I'm fine."

"He had a gun," I said, looking sideways at Niall. He was nodding agreement, and Sam turned to him. "It wasn't loaded," he said. "As soon as the chopper was airborne, Dad opened it and showed me. I don't think he even knows how to use one."

"I'm afraid he does," I said. "At least, he can use a rifle, because when we lived in New Zealand he sometimes went hunting." Not the regular hunting that every local boy does, off into the bush with his first rifle to shoot possum. Possum are Australian animals, and in the New Zealand native forests they do immense damage. They have no natural predators and breed like rabbits. They're officially labelled vermin, and every teenage boy knows he can make decent pocket money by learning how to trap, shoot and skin them. Possum pelts are very soft and can be used for leatherworking, or the fur spun with other fibres to make wool for knitting or weaving.

Drew had never done that – he had no New Zealand family or helpful family friend to introduce him to the art of hunting. Instead, his father paid for him to go on formal hunting trips during school holidays; some to hunt deer or thar in the mountains of the South Island, others to America to learn the art of shooting and take some trophies: big horn sheep and elk. He didn't bring his trophies home – I don't think he especially enjoyed it – but for both Drew and his father, hunting trips were a way to entertain and impress prospective clients.

As a part of their work, hunting was to be done with excellence, like everything else in business. I didn't doubt Drew was an excellent shot with a rifle, and if he decided he needed to use a pistol, he would have paid for training from the best. Nothing is ever done poorly in Drew's world.

"Yeah, but he just wanted to get me to go with him. Once he saw I was co-operating he calmed down and put the gun away. He told me he only wanted to talk. "The chopper took us about an hour's flight away. Dad put a blanket over my head and made me promise not to try and look out. He put a blindfold on me for the last few minutes, so I never saw where we landed."

"A blindfold?" I interjected, disbelievingly.

"Oh yeah." Sam grinned. "The whole James Bond bit. When I took off the blindfold I was in a bedroom – twin beds, like a hotel. There was another room with chairs and a TV, but the outer door was locked. Dad came back a few minutes later with someone else – an old guy in a white suit. If I wasn't so pissed off at the whole thing I'd have laughed. It was looking more and more like the plot of a bad spy film.

"Turns out the white suit dude was some kind of minister. Dad called him Pastor Paul. His job was to turn me away from the darkness of homosexuality and back to the light of a godly life. I must admit, Dad looked a bit sheepish about the God bit. You know he's never gone much on that. He must have been desperate to stop me being gay."

Sam laughed shortly. It wasn't a comfortable sound. He squared his shoulders and looked directly at Niall. "I told him he didn't need to worry: I wasn't gay, or at least I didn't think I was. I said I'd had some feelings that confused me, and the reason I phoned him a few days ago was to see if he could give me some advice. Then, when we started arguing and I felt he was being unreasonable, I only told him I was gay because I knew it would annoy him. I promised him I really liked girls and I wasn't going to 'take the slide into immorality', as Pastor Paul put it."

Sam's eyes hadn't left Niall's. I looked across at him: his

face was grey and his eyes moved, searching Sam's, over and over. Sam smiled again, a rueful, loving, fully adult smile.

"I'll tell Dad whatever he wants to hear, if it means he'll leave me alone to live my life with the man I choose." Once again the two became one, and Sam pressed his forehead against Niall's, the elder still looking uncertain, the younger suddenly in the role of protector.

I felt tears sting my eyes and turned away, giving the two of them a moment of privacy.

"I'm going back to the car," I said. "I think it's going to rain." My mouth was dry, and the words felt hard, like pebbles in my mouth. I wished I could cry, but the ache behind my eyes wasn't going to be eased any time soon. I felt the cold, hard realisation that I was no longer the most important person in my son's life, if indeed I ever had been. He was still the most important in my own, but I would have to learn to shut my mouth and feel that in secret. Last year's fledgling had become a young eagle, taking on the world on his own initiative, and managing to form a deep adult commitment without me even being aware of it. I wasn't needed any more.

I sat in the car, watching a few raindrops crawl down the glass and rubbing the inside of the windscreen with my sleeve when it started to mist up. This is a good thing, I told myself. *It makes Sam happy. I like Niall, and I think I can trust him not to hurt Sam. It's happened, anyway, and can't be undone, so I need to accept it in a quiet, loving way and never let Sam see my doubts and fears.* (This is a good thing, Cas. Get it through your thick head.) I sighed, and rubbed my nose with my wet sleeve. Yeurgh.

A cold draught hit the back of my neck as the doors opened and I shivered as another thought idly crossed my mind. How near had I come to making a pass at Niall? Dear Lord, imagine Niall having to fend off a move from the mother of his boyfriend. I felt sick at the thought of how close I'd been to utter humiliation.

Sam and Niall clambered in and shut the doors, bringing

a wave of damp with them. As I put the key into the ignition my phone chimed the incoming message tone. I glanced down. "Looks like a message from Henry," I said, passing the phone back to Sam. "What does he say?"

"Henry says Bry is getting good results, but he isn't ready to send them off to us yet. He thinks it's the most fun the lab staff have had for ages. They've got a visiting German expert, who has actually seen some of the Dead Sea scrolls, giving them advice on resurrecting text from badly damaged documents, and a Thai lady who did her PhD on the forensic examination of burned documents. But Bry says that realistically it will be at least another fortnight before he has any results to show us."

I twisted round in my seat and looked at my boys, still hand in hand. "Let's get you two back to Tobermory and into that RIB," I said. "I'm not going to relax until I know you've safely back on Lismore and off my hands."

I turned back and began to drive, hearing over the rumble of the engine the quiet murmur of two voices, talking, communicating, and sharing everything. A quick, hot tear stung my eye and I shook my head angrily, hating myself for being so emotionally needy (watch the road, Cas. Concentrate on what's important). Paradoxically, I also felt warmed by a sense of pride in my beautiful, sensible, grown-up son. I was pretty lucky, really.

13

I woke abruptly in the darkness of the short midsummer night, going from sleep to sitting while still only half awake, shaking and covered with sweat. My nightdress clung to my clammy body and my fringe plastered itself down around my temples. I have no idea what I'd been dreaming about, but it must have involved rain because I could still hear it pounding down on the roof, streaming down the windows, looking for a way in through my defences. I still wasn't used to sleeping downstairs, and expected at any moment to feel the cold sensation of water dripping onto my face. As I padded upstairs to the bathroom I kept listening for rain, convinced I must have been woken by the roar of a summer storm battering my roof.

When I got back down to the kitchen and peered out into the pre-dawn twilight all seemed calm, and I could even see a star on the southern horizon. Must have been a dream, then. I made myself a mug of tea and leaned on the counter while I shook the last dregs of sleep out of my head and took stock of the day. Between sips I pottered about, washing last night's few dishes and cleaning the top of the cooker.

The mermaids and lobsters I'd stencilled the year before were already fading into the yellowing wall paint. Was it really only last year I'd been up until midnight painting, trying to make my home look welcoming and, frankly, to make myself look well-off? Trying to create the illusion of prosperity, as if Sam could be fooled by appearances. I thought I'd been quite successful, as Sam had never given any sign that he was aware of quite how bad my financial situation was. I didn't want him to be aware, and if a fresh coat of paint and some distraction activities were necessary to keep him unaware: well, I would just do it all over again for his next visit.

Mind you, last summer I'd been helped by the turmoil in Sam's life, and the allure of our very own archaeological mystery. Still in my dressing gown, I wandered about the living room, dusted photos and the television, and passed the duster over the Calgary Queen. She was looking particularly supercilious this morning, and I paused to consider how my life might appear to an onlooker: no work today, no social arrangements, no urgent work needed on my house despite the parlous state of my roof and walls (which I couldn't afford to fix, anyway). Nobody to notice, frankly, if I fell down in a heap and stopped breathing, right here in my own house. I'd be one of those lonely people who moulder undiscovered for weeks. I laughed scornfully at that – there are plenty of friends available to share their lives with me, and if I could just get a proper job I'd be too busy for such self-pitying thoughts.

In a dozy state of indecision I wandered on, putting my head into the spare room (starting to smell damp. Open window, move boxes around, close door and try not to worry); then into Sam's room (one lost sock and a dried out coffee cup). The bathroom was clean enough, and I wiped down the walls after my shower and bunged some disinfectant into the toilet. My room was also tidy. Too tidy: it's never a good sign when my house is neat. It usually means I've been short of work for some time, as I'd rather do almost anything in preference to housework.

I pulled on a tracksuit and stuffed a piece of buttered toast into my mouth while poking about in the gloomy half-light of the porch looking for my running shoes. Finally, I remembered that they got soaked a couple of weeks ago and I put them on top of the hot water tank to dry out. Had it really been weeks since I last went running?

The morning light was pale and clear, coming through high patchy cloud with pinpricks of stars scattered in the gaps. It gleamed on the drenched grass of the garden and the slick surface of the road. It probably had rained at some point during the night. I warmed up on the road, bending and stretching, finally shaking the night time drowsiness out of my fingertips and setting off.

At first I jogged gently, feeling the stretch in calves and thighs that I'd allowed to stiffen up over two weeks or more of lazy days, but as the muscles warmed I gradually sped up, until I began to feel my breathing quicken and the heat radiate from my brow. I ran to the Torloisk turn-off and back, thinking I would head straight home and call it a day, but on impulse swerved left into the West Ardhu forest track. I jogged through the field, getting soaked to the knees but luckily avoiding an enormous cow pat.

When I reached the forest block I slowed to a walk, struggling to see my footing in the darkness under the trees, but continued to push the pace, leaning on each knee as I took large steps up the steep slope, striding from tree-root to tree-root. As I lunged for the next broad step my foot slipped and I slid sideways, straight onto my right side in a huge puddle of mud that I'd been trying to avoid. I picked myself up and wiped my hands on the left leg of my trousers. The right leg was now soaking and smelled suspiciously of horse. No wonder the track was in such bad shape if it was being used as a bridleway.

I slogged on up the hill, arriving at the top of the forest track at the moment the sun leapt into the sky. From horizon to hill-crest the sky flared blue, the high, thin clouds receding as the summer sun burned through them. It looked as though it was going to be a glorious day.

By the time I hauled myself up onto the giant boulder that lay just below the brow of the hill, I was regretting that I hadn't planned for a day out. I could have done with a quick sip of tea and a sandwich or two, and if I'd had them I think I would have gone on and walked into the hills for the rest of the morning. As it was, I decided to sit in the strengthening sunshine until I dried out. There was nothing in particular for me to do today, and after all the excitement of the last few weeks it was good to sit and think of nothing.

After a while, I turned my back on the pretty view over

Loch Cuin and let the sun fall on my back. I pulled off my scarf and fluffed up my hair to let the sun warm my neck, then settled down with my weight on my left elbow, head on hand, sprawled across the rock.

Before me a short stretch of turf led up to the very top of the hill, where, as I well knew, hill after hill stretched away towards Torloisk and the west coast of Mull. The valleys between the hills were filled with bog and tussocks, covered with the nodding heads of cotton grass and the pale, retiring colours of marshland flowers. Grasses were coming into seed, and over hill and bog subtle shades of yellow and brown were creeping. In a few more weeks, the hills would flush purple with heather, and already I could see patches of brownish pink where the early flowering bell heather was in full bloom.

Right in front of my nose a clump of oxeye daisies stuck out from a rock crevice, and the boulder I sat on was coated with patches of lichen in every shade of brown, red and greenish yellow. We see plenty of sun on Mull, despite its reputation for rain, but it's not always possible to predict when we are going to get it. So a day like this – calm, dry, sunny, and free of plans – is always a precious gift. Who cares about the lack of lunch? I'm going to sit here till my ribs stick to my backbone. I'll feed off the sun like a flower. I'll lie on this rock like a patch of lichen for as long as the sun shines.

I'd no sooner completed the thought than I heard a rattle of rocks falling away to my left. I waited for the blatt of a sheep, but instead my ear caught the sound of breathing. Heavy breathing: human. I sat up and Ewan's head appeared by my knee, as he pulled himself up the last bit of cliff onto the steep side of the rock.

"Hello," I said, forgetting that I wasn't sure whether I was talking to him or not. (Anyway, when in doubt, say something.) "I didn't think there was a path down there." The hill slope to the south of my boulder seat falls away into rough rock and scree. It's a dangerous slope, constantly on the move, and I'd never been down that side of the hill for fear of turning an ankle so far away from help.

"There isn't." As usual Ewan was terse and to-the-point.

I looked at him, my head cocked to one side, and waited. There wasn't any point in jumping in with more questions until he caught his breath, and I'd learned with Ewan that waiting and saying nothing was sometimes the most successful way to get him to communicate. I have to remind myself that the more I talk, the less he needs to speak, so I guarded my tongue and looked around me. I picked one of the oxeye daisies and started to idly pull the petals off it (he loves me, he loves me not. I'm pretty sure he loves me not).

Ewan sat down on the rock beside me and cleared his throat. His breathing was already less ragged. He must have been running hard to have become so breathless. Even when we run together I rarely see him out of breath. A sizeable dribble of blood had dried down his right calf, and I could see that the knee was grazed. There were still dimples in the skin where he'd come down hard on a rough, rocky surface. His legs were long and muscled in his shorts and hiking boots, and I admired them unobtrusively. Then I noticed something else, and I couldn't stop myself speaking: "Where's Molly?"

Ewan started to reply, then cleared his throat and tried again. "Molly's fallen. I was going for help when I saw you up here. Will you come?"

I jumped up and faced him. "Of course. What happened?" He began to lead the way, and I trotted along behind him. We didn't attempt to go straight back down onto the scree, for which I was very thankful. What had he been doing down there anyway? Ewan began to jump from boulder to boulder, but with my shorter legs I was forced to climb down and up again, or push through thick clumps of bracken and goat willow. There was no sign of a track.

I began to fall behind, and pushed myself harder, worrying about what trouble Molly had got herself into. What kind of inaccessible place must she be in, if Ewan had been unable to rescue her on his own?

Distracted, I missed my footing in a patch of soft ground

between boulders and stumbled, grabbing at branches to save myself. A twig scored across my arm and snapped, and as I grasped the foliage to steady myself I smelled the fresh, antiseptic scent of bog myrtle. I pulled off the damaged branch and scrunched up the leaves in my hand, scrubbing the resultant mess over my face and neck, and then into my exposed forearms.

Bog myrtle is said to repel midges and, while I usually rely on something more lethal, it couldn't do any harm. There were no midges around at present – the hill-top breeze and dry air were keeping them away – but the highland midge is a hardy beast, and always on the lookout for a feed. Two panting humans must put out vast quantities of carbon dioxide, which is as good as waving a placard saying 'free blood, come and get it' in midge script.

Ewan stopped and waited for me to catch up. He gestured me to go in front of him, and pointed diagonally across the hill. "That outcrop of rock," he said. I nodded, and started off again. "I went out this morning to check some rabbit snares," he said as he followed close behind me. "Took Molly – needed the walk." I made a noise to show I was listening, but saved my breath for scrambling.

"We were coming back on ourselves, to check the last ones in the line, when Molly fell. She was behind me. I don't know whether the ground gave way beneath her, or she fell and took a pile of rocks with her." Ewan stopped talking, but I didn't need to ask any more. We'd see soon enough what was to be done.

This was the closest we'd come in a long while to a proper conversation, although it was a shame that it had to take an injury to Molly to get him to speak to me. We hadn't talked this much even when Hector was down with pneumonia, although that was probably partly because Ewan had been away during the worst of it, and by the time he got back to Mull Hector was ready to go home and pretend it had never happened.

It was quite possible that Ewan didn't really appreciate how ill Hector had been. The two of them were the healthiest people I'd ever known in my life. Neither of them ever got sick. I knew Hector's illness had hit him hard: he wasn't ready to admit that he was getting old, and a serious illness like that could only remind him of the fact. It was no wonder if he'd hidden the significance of it from Ewan. Probably they were both pretending it would never happen again.

I stopped for a moment, unsure where to put my feet next, and Ewan took the lead again, sidling across the hillside with care. Here was another extensive scree slope, bound by spindly shrubs and patches of scruffy grass. The ground shifted constantly under my feet, and I windmilled my arms to try and keep my balance. I suppose it was a good place to set snares – little chance of any other hunter bothering to come up here and check your traps, and zero chance of accidentally catching a tourist's dog – but I couldn't imagine what any self-respecting rabbit would be doing here either.

The slope ended at a vast outcropping of weathered basalt, crumbling and treacherous, and the rocks we had disturbed during our descent pinged out into empty space, landing seconds later with faint sounds below. Ewan gripped my arm and I leaned over the cliff and looked down. There was Molly, her reddish fur blending with the rusty iron colours of the rocks on which she lay. Lumps of rock lay on her too. It looked as though she'd taken part of the cliff with her as she fell.

"Molly, lass," I called, and she raised her head. Still alive then. A wave of relief passed over me, but immediately I became aware of something disturbing. I looked at her carefully. Something about the way she was lying? Then I realised: she hadn't wagged her tail. Molly always does when she greets you. Even when she's lying comatose by Hector's fire, and getting up to greet visitors is the last thing on her mind, she always lifts her head and gives one thump of her tail, before returning to her dreaming in front of the embers.

Ewan whistled – his come-hither call. Molly raised her

head again, and gave a faint whine. I was right. Her tail didn't move. And the shape of her lying there didn't look right either. I had a feeling she might not have any movement in her hindquarters at all.

I moved back from the edge and looked at Ewan. He nodded his agreement with my concerned expression. Neither of us spoke for a moment. I think we both knew how serious the situation was.

"I'm going down," he said. "Don't come after me. If anything happens to me, I'll need you to go for help."

He handed me his backpack before turning to the right and beginning to pick his way around the edge of the cliff, swearing briefly under his breath as a lump of rock broke away at his feet and skittered off the cliff. I went down onto hands and knees to peer out over the edge, but the rockfall had missed the dog, who was now lying unmoving and seemingly unaware of the human drama playing out above her head.

"She's okay," I said, as his worried face turned briefly towards me.

I held my breath as Ewan made his careful, painstaking way down the hillside and round to the place where Molly lay. He knelt beside her and gripped her ruff. She roused then and, lifting her head, looked at him, but only for a moment before letting it fall again.

Ewan stood and looked around. He turned and craned his head to look at me, and then gestured towards the north. I gave him a thumbs-up. He bent and carefully lifted Molly, cradling her in his arms. As soon as he did so, I could see there was something wrong with her hindquarters. Her legs didn't hang right, and they seemed strangely elongated. It was clear she didn't have any movement there at all, because her front legs scrabbled on the stones as Ewan strove to raise her, but her back paws hung limply and her tail didn't even twitch. Ewan began to shuffle sideways, out from under the cliff and back up the hill.

It seemed to take forever for the two of them to make any progress. After a while they got onto slightly firmer ground, and I made my way gingerly down to meet them. Ewan shook his head at my wordless offer of help, and set off steadily. I brought up the rear, trying not to feel useless. This time when we crossed the boulder field he did not jump from rock to rock, but let himself down and up again with great care, trying not to jostle Molly as we made our way. I could see a clear route to the hill crest now and took the lead, stopping every now and again to help steady Molly as Ewan climbed.

At last we made it back to the big boulder where I had reclined so peacefully that morning. Ewan set Molly down carefully on its lichen-coated surface and I pulled a flask of water out of his pack. We got a warmish mouthful each, and then he tried to give Molly some from his cupped hand. She was barely conscious and wouldn't drink, so he dripped the water slowly into her mouth. A moment later she swallowed convulsively and we looked at one another, relieved, but the next mouthful dripped off her tongue and onto the rock.

Ewan handed me his pack again and I pulled it on, while he lifted Molly and adjusted his balance. The walk back down seemed interminable, and even when we hit the road and turned for home Ewan refused to stop. By the time we came abreast of my gate the sweat was dripping off him.

"Will I call the vet from here?" I asked him, but he didn't reply. He just kept on putting one foot in front of the other, steady and slow, with the body of the dog held before him like an offering. I followed on behind, still carrying his pack, until we reached the turnoff to Hector's house. Down the drive, through the gate, past the caravan and up onto the mossy porch of the house. I reached past Ewan and opened the door, and the slow steps continued into the parlour. There, at last, he knelt down and gently deposited his burden on the rug in front of the fireplace.

Hector had risen to his feet when we entered the room, but like his son he said nothing. He knelt down next to Molly and laid his hand on her head. The old eyes flickered open and her muzzle raised to him. Hector looked up and his eyes met Ewan's. Still no word had been exchanged. I held my breath and waited.

"She fell," said Ewan at last. His voice rasped. He was still catching his breath. "Dad, I think she broke her back."

Hector bowed his head. His face remained expressionless, but a tear gathered and dripped slowly down his nose to fall onto Molly's fur. His hand stayed on her head, stroking and stroking, so gently. He looked across to me and smiled sweetly, all his love for the dog in his eyes. "Call the vet, lass," he said. "The red book is in the drawer."

14

The phone rang and rang and wasn't answered. That's quite normal for the vet, although I'd hoped it would go to answerphone. I tried again, and again it rang on, but this time it was answered, just as I was about to hang up again. I explained about Molly as best I could, then walked back to the front room to pass on the message.

Hector's chair had been dragged to the fireside, and he sat forward, one hand still resting on Molly's head. Ewan perched beside him on a kitchen chair; they raised their heads in unison to look at me as I came through the door. Molly lay unmoving, but the skin of her muzzle twitched a little.

"The vet's on a farm visit near Salen," I told them. "They think they can get hold of her, and she'll come round here when she's finished, but she might be an hour or two."

Ewan patted Molly carefully and pulled himself to his feet. He went silently out of the room, and a moment later I heard the door close behind him. Hector nodded at me and smiled his thanks.

"Tea?" I asked.

"Yes, thank you, lass." Hector's voice was soft with unshed tears. I felt mine well up in response, and blinked them away as I turned away towards the kitchen. I heard the front door go again as the kettle came to the boil, and made up three mugs of strong tea. As I stirred hard to dissolve the four teaspoons of sugar that Ewan takes, I heard low voices in the front room. Ewan was back in his seat beside Hector, the two heads together as they bent over the dog. I caught my breath for a moment, but Molly's tummy rose and fell and I breathed along with her.

I handed out the mugs and sank into the other armchair,

an old, brown, tweedy thing with wooden legs, well chewed from the days when Molly had been a puppy. How old was she? I thought back to my first meeting with Hector, leaning on his gate in the summer sunshine, and all the times since then that I'd met the old man and his dog, out in his garden, or over at the shops. Molly and Hector had become a part of our lives. It was impossible to imagine they wouldn't always be there.

I loved my weeks in the summer house. Drew would come and go, flying back for business meetings, or arranging charter yachts out of Tobermory or Oban to impress prospective clients. Sam lay in bed every morning, saving his energies for afternoon football with the local boys, and staying up as late as possible every night. That left me free to walk out after breakfast, and know I was not needed until lunchtime.

It was a freedom I relished, and eventually it gave me the impetus to take up running again. I'd run in High School, though I'd not been in the top echelon of sporty pupils, and although it was hard at first I soon found my wind and enjoyed pounding the roads and tracks of Mull, knowing that a mug of tea would be waiting for me at Hector's if I headed in that direction at the end of my run.

It was on one of my longer runs that I bumped into Molly, sitting by the track, bright eyed with her tongue hanging out, looking as though she was having a marvellous day. I sank down beside her and ruffled her fur, and she panted up at me with a gleam in her eye. I heard a shrill whistle (which Molly ignored) and a moment later Ewan came round the corner, heading down the hill. He pulled up beside us and frowned at Molly. "Cheeky bitch," he muttered.

I started at that, but of course he wasn't talking to me. Or was he? I glanced up at him and he avoided my gaze, although a smile twitched at the corner of his mouth. "Coming to Dad's?" he asked, setting off again and gesturing to Molly, who came to heel. It seemed only natural to fall in behind him down the track, and to run beside him to Hector's, who greeted us as if seeing us together was of no moment. We never made any arrangement to run together, but it was surprising how often I could take off at some unplanned time, in a direction I was sure was random, and bump into Ewan and Molly at some point during the run.

I sipped my tea and looked across at my friends, father and son. Molly had been old even then, grey in the muzzle, and rather fond of lying in front of the fire, even when it wasn't lit. Whether she'd been a working dog in her youth I didn't know, but she had certainly been an old man's pet for several years. Probably her runs with Ewan had provided some of the fitness training that had kept her alive for so long.

A thought occurred to me, and I chewed it over, smiling wryly to myself. I wondered whether all those fortuitous meetings with Ewan had been so accidental after all. I liked Molly, and the feeling seemed to be mutual, especially as I often had a doggy treat in my pocket for her. It would not have been difficult to track me down if you were running with Molly.

A vehicle hooted outside and Ewan jumped up. If it was the vet she would need someone to open the gate. I looked across to Molly; she was breathing even more shallowly if possible, and seemed to be asleep or unconscious. Ewan came back in, holding the door for Tina MacDonald. She was mousy-haired, slender and tiny. An astonishingly unlikely looking vet, she had a broad and busy practice with both small animals and livestock. She knelt beside Molly and opened her bag, beginning her inspection by peering into one of the dog's eyes and then taking a pulse.

She worked quietly and competently, and while she did so gently persuaded Ewan to tell her in full detail what had happened that morning. It was more than he'd told me, and I looked at her curiously. She was neither demanding nor bossy, and yet without difficulty she persuaded him to flesh out the bare bones of the story. She nodded at just the right intervals, but otherwise listened quietly as she went about her business.

Molly had been behind Ewan when she fell, so he hadn't seen her go over. In fact, he hadn't been aware quite how near to the cliff edge he was. He thought perhaps Molly was walking even closer to the edge than he was, and he wondered if she had been trying to drive him inward, protecting him from the drop. His first warning of trouble came when the dog yelped, and when he turned he saw nothing but some loose stones tumbling over the edge amid the red dust of a major rock fall.

He'd had to wait until the dust cleared before he could see Molly, and when he did it was clear he would have to go for help. "No point in falling myself, and no-one to know where," he ended, voice cracking on the last word. Hector patted his son on the arm, but Ewan seemed unaware. "I should have taken more care," he ended, miserably.

Tina MacDonald had worked her way from one end of the dog to the other, and was palpating the hind limbs and spine. She smoothed out Molly's tail, and ran her hands down the long back, firmly but gently. Then she pulled out a tiny torch and took a much more careful look in Molly's eyes, shifting around on her knees to get different angles of light. She sat back on her heels and looked up at Hector and Ewan.

"You haven't done anything wrong," she reassured them. "It wasn't your fault. You're right that Molly appears to have lost function in her hindquarters, but I don't think it's a result of injury. Amazingly, she has no broken bones, and I can't feel any abnormality in the spine. I think she's had a stroke. Most likely, the yelp you heard was the moment the stroke hit. It caused her to fall, and part of the cliff broke off as she went. But the stroke preceded the fall, I'm sure of it."

Ewan's eyes were bright and wide open as he forced back tears, and he finally seemed to notice Hector's patting hand. He took his father's hands in his own and looked him in the eye. Hector rested his gnarled hands in the large, strong ones of his son, turned back to Tina and asked, "What are her chances?"

Tina's smile was compassionate as she replied, "I'm afraid there's nothing more I can do. It was a very severe stroke, and substantial loss of function has resulted. Molly may last a day or two, but she is dying. If you wish, I can put her down now, but at the moment she isn't in any pain."

The old man and the younger one sat speechless for a moment and we all waited, the only sound in the room the ticking of the clock and the shallow, panting breath of the old dog. Then Hector stirred himself. "If we let you go, and she's taken bad again, we may not be able to get you back in time. Do your job, Tina. It's time for her to go."

Tina stood and gathered her equipment." I'll get the stuff from the truck," she said, and carried her bag outside. I looked after her, puzzled. That was a big, well-organised bag; I found it hard to believe that she didn't carry everything she needed in there. Perhaps the euthanasia stuff has to be kept locked up separately?

Then I looked at the two men, now both on their knees fondling the old dog, Hector moving her head slightly, trying to make her last moments as comfortable as they possibly could. I suspected that Tina had the drug in her bag all along. With exquisite compassion, she'd given them the privacy they need to say goodbye before the needle came out. I looked at the doorway, appreciating the subtlety of the woman, and recognised I had something to learn from that. My attention was drawn back to the tableau in the room, where Molly had opened her eyes and was licking Hector's fingers.

"Good lass," he said, stroking her head. "There's a good lass, now."

Molly whined deep in her throat and gave a sharp yip. Then her head fell back and she seemed to twitch slightly. Hector sighed, in an echo of his dog's whine, and bowed his head. I was still listening for the return of the vet when I realised that Molly's eyes were open, and they were clouding over. It seemed Tina's intervention wouldn't be needed after all.

Hector reached for his son, and Ewan helped him to his

feet. Before Ewan could move away, Hector embraced him. Ewan stood stiffly for a moment, and then his arms came forward and he held the old man tightly, head bowed over his father's as they stood together. After a moment he stepped back, and Hector bent to stroke his dog for the last time.

15

Over the next few days I tried to pop in to see Hector every day. Ewan buried the dog in the back garden, over in the corner near the old plum tree. He'd picked a hard corner to dig, but he was determined, and spent all his waking time thumping away at the ground and carving out bits of root until the hole was deep enough. He had no words for us, and when I expressed my concern to Hector he told me to "leave the boy be." Hector believed that Ewan still blamed himself, and I rehearsed all the arguments that I knew Ewan wouldn't be able to hear from me: the vet had told us her death was due to a stroke, and not to a fall, and anyway it wasn't Ewan's fault even if it was the fall.

"I know that," said Hector, patting my arm comfortingly, "but the boy needs to do this. He'll come right, don't worry."

I don't know if they held any ceremony. The burial was done quietly and privately, and only Hector and Ewan know what went on, but afterwards Ewan seemed relieved. A couple of days later, he went off working. I took to cooking extra food and taking care packages round to Hector, but when I realised he wasn't eating the meals I was carefully preparing for him, I told him I was going to come and cook for him at the house each day.

Hector made the effort to be sociable with me while I was there, but clearly it was an effort, and I was sure that when I wasn't there he would sink down into his chair beside the cold fire side and sit for hours, alone now as he'd never been before. I racked my brains for things to do for him, offered to take him for a drive, shopping in Tobermory, maybe a trip to Oban. Hector just wanted to be left alone. He would at least eat if I sat with him and ate as well.

Simple courtesy meant he couldn't refuse while I sat there in front of him, but I don't believe he tasted any of it. It was going to be the best part of a week till Ewan got back and I couldn't think what to do.

Then it struck me. I knew who to call: someone who always knows what to do in a crisis. I got on the phone to Bernie and told all. Bernie was sharp with me. Who was I to dictate how someone else handled their grief? If Hector wanted to be left alone, perhaps that was just what he needed. But she did agree that he ought not to be alone all the time. I left her thinking about it.

That afternoon, as I arrived at Hector's armed with a container of home-made soup, I found Jed's battered Land Rover standing in the yard. He was sitting on the porch having a sneaky smoke (Jed fondly believed that Bernie didn't know he still occasionally smoked). From the interior I could hear Tom's voice, clear and high, and a faint rumble from Hector. A moment later, a boy and a black and white furry object pounded past me and into the garden. Hector shuffled to the door in his slippers and greeted us. "Can't keep up with the young any more."

Jed grinned at him. Then he sobered and stood. "Sorry to hear about your Molly," he said.

Hector shrugged placidly. "It was her time," he said.

"How old was she?"

"I had her from a puppy. Eighteen years."

Jed nodded. "A good age." We looked out over the garden where the furry object had resolved itself into something with legs that was barking wildly and chasing sticks that Tom was throwing for it.

"Old English Sheepdog, looks like to me," said Hector.

"Yes. At least, we think Old English Sheepdog/Collie cross," said Jed. "Only six months old. Came from the rescue centre in Inverness. He's going to be huge."

"What do you call him?" I asked.

"Well, that depends on who you ask. Tom claims his name is Reggae. Tilly wants to call him Barkley. Bernie generally refers to him as 'That Damn Dog'. I'm still thinking about it."

"Reggie?" I said.

"No, Reggae. Like the music."

Jed looked at us both and shrugged. "Nope, I don't get it either." He stood up and cupped his hands round his mouth. "Tom, it's time to go."

Jed turned to Hector, who was smiling at the antics of the boy as he tried to get hold of his dog and calm it down enough to get the lead on. "You should think about getting another dog," he said. "I could put the word out."

"Oh, no, I won't get another." Hector was adamant. "I'm too old to think about training up a puppy. Leave that to young pups like your Tom." The young pup came running up with his dog in tow, and skidded to a halt in front of Hector.

"Thank you for the biscuits," he said.

"You're very welcome," said the old man, gravely.

"Next time will you teach me that trick with the wee ball?" pleaded Tom. "You know: the one you taught to Molly?"

I winced at this open assault on the painful memory, but Hector smiled and ruffled Tom's hair. "I'd love to," he said. "You bring back that monster another day and we'll see if he's got a brain in his head."

Tom and Reggae dashed off in the direction of the car, although it wasn't exactly clear which of them was leading. Jed shook Hector's hand and offered me a hug. "Abyssinia," he said, tucking his tobacco pouch safely away in his back pocket, and ambled off after his son.

Hector and I sat peaceably while the soup cooked itself, and we shared a quiet meal together on the porch as the sun went down. We went in as the midges started to bite, and I put the kettle on for a cuppa before heading home. Hector pulled down a tin from the shelf and opened the lid to reveal that it was crammed full of homemade shortbread biscuits. I looked at him and we both laughed.

"Tom told me his Mum cooked too many."

"Mmm hmm," I mumbled, through a mouthful of biscuit.

Hector put the tin away again, and turned to pour the tea.

"I'm going to be all right, you know," he told me.

"I know that."

"That soup'll keep me going for a day or two. And before you know it Ewan will be back. You don't need to bring me any more meals. It's always nice to see you, though."

I took a leaf out of Bernie's book, and told myself to recognise the distinction between caring about someone and taking over their life. "You're always welcome, Hector," I said. "Don't be a stranger."

"Strangers are only friends you haven't met yet, and we have been friends for a long time, Cassandra Longmore."

I felt tears prickle the backs of my eyes again as I closed the gate and started the walk home, but this time I let them fall. I couldn't work out if I was crying for Molly who was dead, for Hector who had lost her, or for me – going back to my empty home, where nobody needed me. I shook myself savagely and ran the rest of the way home. Tomorrow I would air out the spare room and scrub the walls ready for a coat of paint. I'd ring round to see if anyone had work for me. I needed to come up with a bit of money to buy some paint, then we'd see how nice I could make the place look.

Perhaps it was a coincidence to find a letter on the mat from the Scottish Archaeological Finds and Allocations Panel. They wanted to know my bank details so they could make me an ex gratia payment in exchange for the Calgary Chess Queen. Paint for sure, then. I tucked the envelope in beside the Chess Queen, who was looking remarkably smug. I wondered if there would be enough for the roof materials as well.

16

So much for domestic plans. I got home to find two messages on my phone. The first was from Bernie, who announced she had some work for me. The second was from Niall – would I please call him back? Not very informative, either of them. I called Bernie first. I could hardly hear her over the sound of a very distressed baby.

She admitted she was knee-deep in the week's laundry, the tumble-dryer had broken down and the baby was teething. She had a proposal for me. Would I agree to paint Tom and Tilly's bedrooms, and the shed, in return for Jed fixing the remaining urgent problems with my house. I told her that was daft: she was perfectly capable of doing a bit of painting. I reminded her how I'd sat and watched her redecorate the nursery ready for Emma Jane.

"That's not the point," my friend retorted. "I don't have the energy or desire to paint at the moment, it's Jed's busy season and Mum's gone away to visit her sister. In order for me to paint, I'd have to pay someone to babysit, and I know which job I'd rather be doing. Plus I'm being very cheeky, because I'm not offering you actual money. Hopefully this benefits both of us."

I had to admit she had a point. I told her I thought it was a great idea and I'd be over tomorrow to get started. That left Niall. I wondered what on earth could be the matter this time. Was there trouble with Drew again? Something new at the dig? (Just call him, woman. Save the worrying till after you find out what's going on.)

As it turned out the news was all good; the dig was going from strength to strength. The girls' team hadn't found any more bodies, but they were busy perfecting their notes on the ones they had. John had started a new test pit with Rick and Lily, based on a particularly promising spike in the geophysics results, and they'd immediately hit pay dirt: a stone socket, of the kind that might well have held a large cross, and associated with it a collection of white pebbles. "Textbook stuff," said Niall, delighting in the successes of his team.

"We've heard from Bryan in London. The forensics results are almost complete, but he's offered me the opportunity to go down to London and see the lab for myself. He says he can show me what he's found in greater detail if we view it on his equipment. It's a great chance for me to learn more about his area of expertise.

"The problem is that I have to be back here in three days to close down the dig and finalise the students' workbooks, and that will mean driving through the night to get down there, and turning straight round to drive back again the following night. Would you consider coming with me to share the driving? If not, then I'll go alone, but if I have a second driver with me then I can offer Sam the chance to come as well."

"Put like that, how can I refuse?" I said. "Anyway, I've never met Bry. I'd like to see who Marise has chosen. Are you sure you don't want to stay over one night? Henry would gladly put us up."

"I'm sorry, Cas. I really want to be back for the final day of the dig. The kids deserve a proper post-mortem from me, and if I have the results of Bry's analysis to give them it will just about make their year. Lisbet is already crowing that it's the best dig she's ever been on, although I think that's as much to do with the weather as the archaeology."

I laughed. It has been the loveliest summer. Enough rain to keep things growing, but not too much, and cool enough on some days to make the warm days feel really good by comparison. "What's your plan of action?" I asked.

"Can you meet me in Oban tonight off the five o'clock ferry? We'll come off Lismore on the four-thirty and meet you at the terminal. I've arranged to meet Bryan at eleven tomorrow morning, which should give us several hours to talk things over with him, have a meal and a brief respite before we head back."

I glanced at the clock. I had enough time if I sprinted. "Done," I said. "I'll see you there."

"Thanks, Cas, you're brilliant."

I ran upstairs and picked up the bag of bits I'd bought when I overnighted in Tobermory. The bag was still lying in the corner of the bedroom where I'd dropped it. I added a clean top, picked up my toothbrush and deodorant from the bathroom and took a quick look at myself in the mirror. The bruises on my neck were already fading, though I was still intending to wear blouses with collars for a while. I smoothed a little foundation cream over them and added the bottle to my bag of essentials.

Actually, the dark circles under my eyes were more obvious than the bruises Drew had caused. I closed my eyes and let my breathing slow; trying to empty my mind, but my inner voice reminded me that I didn't have time. Not for the first time, I made myself a mental promise to start meditating again.

With one last check in the mirror to make sure the bruises were not visible, I ran downstairs, grabbed my purse and keys from the kitchen and snatched up my lightest coat from the porch. At the last minute I remembered to take my mobile phone (actually charged up, for a change) and raced off to Craignure. I made it with plenty of time to spare – at least five minutes. I parked in the long-stay car park, and once I'd got myself settled in the ferry's passenger lounge I phoned Bernie.

"Sorry, my love, I can't come tomorrow. Something's come up and I've had to sprint off to London."

"London? What is it? Is everything okay?"

"Yeah, no problem. Niall needs a second driver to get him to London by eleven tomorrow morning, and I've been volunteered. We're going to collect the forensic results on the bit of stuff the mummified hand was holding."

"Urghh." Bernie was squeamish about my latest adventure. I suppose I couldn't blame her. I'd felt a bit queasy myself when Niall first made the discovery. "I've been worried about you," Bernie said.

"What? Why?"

"Just that I haven't seen you for a few weeks, and the last time we talked on the phone you seemed a bit…off. I know you were upset about Molly, but are you sure there isn't anything else?"

"I don't know what you mean." I fingered the bruises under my collar. Sooner or later I'd tell Bernie. I told her everything. It was just that I couldn't work out how to start.

"I should be back before the weekend. Is it okay if I start the painting then?"

"You start the painting whenever you like," said Bernie. "It's not a big deal, but I'd hoped Jed could take a proper look at your roof tomorrow. He reckons he's got everything he needs to put it right."

"The spare key's under the rain barrel. He can let himself in. In fact, could you ask him to check that I turned off the cooker?"

"Sure. You know you did, though. You always get paranoid about it. I'll tell Jed he can get stuck into your roof, and by the time you get home you'll owe me good."

"That's cool, as my son hates to hear me say."

"Speaking of your son, how's he getting on in his new career? Is your Niall Webster being good to him?"

I opened my mouth to reply and was hit by a fit of coughing. Bernie waited patiently until I got myself sorted before she spoke. "Auntie Bernie perceives a story."

"Auntie Bernie doesn't know the half of it. He's having a great time, and I've got lots of gossip for you. I promise to tell all as soon as I get back."

"You'd better," she said. "Gossip is my lifeblood and with Mum away I'm starved of my usual titbits about the Women's Auxiliary and the Gaelic Choir. I'm desperate for some juicy news. You can paint and talk at the same time."

Still laughing, I signed off and sat back to watch the view from the ferry. As we passed Lismore lighthouse I looked across and glimpsed Annaid's tiny beach, and a sliver of red roof behind the hill. I strained my eyes to see the tumbledown building where we'd found the kist, but I couldn't make it out against the grey rocks of the cliff.

Were any of the team working there today? Or had their discoveries at Achnacroish put a stop to Niall's plans to extend the dig to the south of the island? If I knew Niall, he'd probably already put in grant applications to fund a dig at Annaid next summer. I leaned back and closed my eyes – time for a few winks to prepare myself for the night ahead.

17

The journey went off without incident. Niall drove first, and I took the middle shift, with Sam snoring on the back seat. The hardest part was finding somewhere to park once we got into the city, but we managed to find a space in an underground car park within half an hour's walk of the lab, and in the end we were only a few minutes late. Bry met us at the front door and escorted us through the building until we reached a large laboratory. He threw his suit jacket over the back of a chair and invited us in.

The lab smelled of chemicals. Not the bleach and boiled-cabbage smell of hospitals, and in fact the scent was very faint, but definitely reminiscent of my secondary school chemistry lab. I breathed in through my nose and the smell was gone, leaving the everyday air of an everyday room; except that the room was full of tall benches, sinks, white Formica-topped tables, an autoclave, a big first aid cupboard, computers, a laptop perched on top of a pile of files in one corner, some stools pushed together in another. Everything was scrupulously clean, but with a friendly sense of disorder. I pinched my nose between my fingers and breathed through my mouth for a moment, then sniffed again. Definitely a faint chemical twang.

Across the room on a high bench were two wires sticking out of lumps of plasticine. On top of the wires two minute clothes pegs were attached, and they held between them a tiny scrap of brownish fabric. A tall glass dome had been placed over the whole ensemble. Niall was immediately interested: "That's a lovely bit of glass," he said, examining it closely. "Nineteenth century clock case, it looks like. I thought it was generally the clock that survived and the case that was lost?"

"You're right," said Bry, "I still have the clock, but it's in pieces. I needed a dust cover for this piece, so I could go back and look at it while we were waiting for test results, and this was perfect. Actually, you can still buy glass domes – there are a couple of internet companies that supply them – but this was lying around at home, so I brought it in."

"What happened to the clock?" asked Niall. I was twitching impatiently. Who cares about old clocks? When were we going to get to the archaeology?

"It used to belong to my grandfather. Strictly speaking it should have gone to Roddie, as the whole estate was entailed, but Roddie knew the old man wanted me to have it. It hasn't worked for decades, but when I was a sprog I was forever taking off the dome and fiddling with it, trying to make it work.

"Eventually the inevitable happened. The dome was safely on the sideboard, but I tried to lift the clock and dropped it. Bits came spanging out all over the rug. I was in a power of trouble – could hardly sit down for a week, and the old man nearly broke his cane on my cast iron backside. Afterwards he shoved all the bits back under the dome and walked away. I never dared touch it again, and I always felt guilty.

"When he died, Roddie told me I was to have the clock, just as it was. I can't decide whether it was a generous gift (it was moderately valuable before I broke it) or one of the old man's typical twisted jokes, giving me the thing I'd ruined. Anyway, it really is in bits now and I'm slowly piecing it back together."

I nodded sympathetically. "You must have been disappointed, if your brother got everything else and you only got a broken clock."

Bry snorted. "Nah. At least he didn't give me the house. Poor Roddie. He has to spend all his time earning enough money to stop the roof from falling in, and he has to live with a pile of mathoms that he's too sentimental to get rid of. Family heirlooms, my arse."

I'd never looked at it that way before. Entailed estates

seem so unfair, when the eldest male heir inherits the lot and younger sibs are left with nothing. I thought about Bry and Marise's easy, double-income-no-kids lifestyle; and Henry's comments about Bry. He had been scathing about Bry's choice of career. "Son of a peer's daughter, and he decides to be a policeman." It cut no ice with Henry that forensic science required a good degree or two and a sharp, incisive intelligence. Nor that not all the work Bryan did was for the police (hence his involvement with our artefact).

It seemed to me, though, that Bry had made some sensible choices. He still had his ancestors if he wanted to make anything of them, but his income and lifestyle were wholly independent of his family connection. Maybe the younger son gets a better deal, even if he doesn't have the title and the estate. Especially if the estate is a mouldering old house that's falling apart, and isn't worth enough to be of interest to Russian oligarchs or national heritage organisations.

Bry lifted the glass dome carefully off his exhibit and handed Niall a magnifying glass. "You wouldn't believe the amount of trouble you've put me to," he said happily. "I hope your credit's good at the bank because you've spent a small mortgage." I glanced quickly at Niall, but his face was sanguine. He bent over the scrap and examined it closely. At last he sighed happily and passed the glass to me. "You've done a lovely job," he said. "I wouldn't have expected it to come out so well. What did you do?"

"Well, to start with we had to stabilise it, make sure it wasn't going to degrade once it was exposed to the air. We've been keeping it in a sealed chamber, maintaining the atmosphere in homeostatic balance with the piece. That's one reason I brought in the dome – so we could minimise the risk of deterioration when we have to take it out of the cabinet."

I'd been peering through the magnifying glass at nothing very much. As far as I could see, the scrap, although now brown rather than black, conveyed hardly more information than when it had still been clenched in the mummified fist. I could see some patches of reddish and yellowish discolouration, making the piece look rather mouldy, and there was one dark, curving vertical line and a few fainter marks. I handed the glass to Sam to see if he could make anything of it.

"Sealed chamber?" I asked. "Sounds like something from the pharaoh's tomb."

Bry laughed. "Well, really it's a glorified fume cupboard," he admitted. "We have a couple of high-end ones which don't vent outside the building – the exchange of air can be controlled from the lab. They're vented through a dense carbon matrix, which absorbs any harmful gases produced by whatever experiment we're performing. It wasn't difficult to modify one to prevent any exchange of atmosphere. And, of course, they are temperature-controlled. The only time the item is vulnerable is when it's removed from the cabinet and exposed to the air in the lab. Hence the dome."

Bry picked up the dome and its contents and carried them a few feet to a glass-fronted cupboard set into the wall. He keyed in a code and the glass front slid upwards, allowing him to place the dome inside. The ceiling of the cupboard was so high that he was able to lift the dome right off the display and remove it. Then he slid the door back down and used a key code to lock it. He checked a display set into the door surround, picked up a clipboard that was hanging next to it, and made a note of the temperature and humidity inside.

"Looks as though our item is in good hands," said Niall, pleased. "Why don't we go and get a coffee, and you can tell me exactly what has just cost me my grandmother's inheritance."

Bry straightened his waistcoat and draped his suit jacket over his shoulders. He collected the laptop from the top of its pile of papers and, tucking it under his arm, gestured for us to precede him. "I have to say I'm surprised," remarked Niall. "I thought you scientist types always wore a white lab coat."

Bry snorted. "It's not compulsory, you know. I wear one when I think my suit's going to get damaged, or when safety regs require it, but by and large the only lab coats you see around here belong to the technicians."

"Like that one," I said, indicating a petite blonde who had entered the room with a clipboard in her hand. She was well groomed and exquisitely made up, with a perfectly styled elfin cut, wearing slim-fitting trousers and flat shoes under an immaculately clean white coat. Seeing her immediately made me feel scruffy, ungainly and slightly grubby. Bry looked round.

"Oh, no, no, no," he said, grinning. "That's the boss." He raised his voice slightly. "Professor Mallory?"

The woman crossed the lab to join us. "Hello Bryan," she said. "Hello," nodding to us.

"This is Niall Webster," said Bry, "our latest patron. And Cassandra and Sam Longmore. Niall, Cas, Sam: please meet Professor Jennifer Mallory, our director."

"Pleased to meet you," we said, shaking hands all round.

"Doctor Mallory will do fine," said the blonde vision, frowning slightly at Bry. "I'm only 'Professor' to my students at the university. I think you've already learned pretty much everything I can teach you."

"She means I'm incapable of learning anything more," interjected Bry, and she laughed.

"I only keep him on for his comic qualities," she said. Bry mimed a wounding blow to the heart and she continued, "Did you get anywhere with the X-ray fluorescence?"

"No, that wasn't great. I did better with the infrared luminosity. I'm about to run through the results with the client."

"Good. I'll leave you to it. Drop your report in to my office this afternoon and I'll look at it over the weekend."

"Sure."

The petite blonde whisked away to the far end of the room and began to make notes on her clipboard, while Bry led the way down to the street and round the corner to a small cafe. After we were all settled with our choice of caffeine-based products, he opened up the laptop and spun it round to face Niall.

"You can see from the natural light photographs that there was really no visible information on the untreated piece." Right enough, it was just a black blob on the screen, much as I remembered it emerging from the hand of its long-dead owner. "Had the piece been in better condition, or less valuable, there are a number of treatments we could have given it to flatten out the vellum, make any markings more visible and even help to preserve it. But the piece was so tiny and fragile that we initially elected not to take any irreversible measures. Many of the techniques we could have used ran an appreciable risk of destroying the piece." Niall nodded and gestured to Bry to continue, but I didn't understand.

"How can you learn anything without treating the piece to get rid of the burning? In these pictures it doesn't look any different to when it was first discovered."

"There are a number of investigations we can carry out while minimising handling of the artefact. Many of them were developed during study of the Dead Sea scrolls. You may remember that the Dead Sea scrolls were found near the Dead Sea in Jordan, around the middle of last century. They were probably written during the last two hundred years BCE, and they're of great interest to archaeologists and students of early Christianity, because some of them contain alternative gospels as well as a wealth of other information about the period."

"What's BCE?" I asked.

"Before the Common Era – it's what used to be known as B.C." He went on. "The Dead Sea scrolls are very delicate. Each contains a potentially unique record which is not visible to the eye because the scrolls are rolled up. Opening a scroll does irreversible damage, and each scroll can only be opened a finite number of times before it disintegrates. So a battery of procedures was developed that allow scientist to read the scrolls without unrolling them, even if they have text on both sides.

"Some of those techniques have proven to be very helpful in examining the Lismore fragment."

"So you do think it's a fragment of a larger work?" asked Niall.

"Absolutely. To begin with we photographed it in various levels of natural light, with fibre-optic backlighting, which allows us to get some sense of the type of fabric the fragment is made from. That told us we were almost certainly dealing with a piece of very fine vellum. Vellum is the inner layer of skin from a calf, and it has unique characteristics which distinguish it from parchment made of the skin of older animals, however fine, and also from plant-pulp products such as paper.

"Even using the best image-analysing software available, we couldn't make much of the surface markings, so we started again using X-ray and ultraviolet fluorescence techniques. That involves photographing the piece under various wavelengths of light that are shorter than the visible spectrum. We were able to conclusively show that there were markings, that they looked as though they may be writing, and that the main ink used is very high in iron. Our best guess is oak gall ink, which was known to be used in monastic writing throughout the Celtic church during the Dark Ages.

"We can't get a firm date for your piece. Dating processes would require the whole piece to be destroyed, and there's no guarantee we would get a clear date anyway, but the best information came from infrared luminescence: photography using very long wavelengths of light."

As Bry spoke, he flicked his way through a series of photographs, of a dark blob, a slightly less dark blob, a greyish mass with indistinct markings, a brownish lump on a brownish screen. Niall and Sam leaned forward to peer eagerly at each one, but I couldn't see that they looked significantly different from one another. Then Bry opened a page that made even me move in for a closer look. The image was in shades of greenish grey, but the detail was so sharp that the little pegs holding the fragment up were clearly visible. The fragment itself seemed to glow, and from the darkness around it emerged the lines and curls of Celtic style handwriting. Suddenly, the little burned object had a story to tell.

Niall frowned, concentrating. "In…" he muttered. "Then there's a 'p', and a 'v'. Further down it looks like 'ap'." His face cleared and he looked up at us, glowing with delight. "In principio erat Verbum et Verbum erat apud Deum et Deus erat Verbum."

He stared from one face to the other, nodding impatiently. "Come on, Bry, surely you studied Latin at school."

"Fell asleep in every lesson," Bry admitted. "Go on then, impress us some more."

"In the beginning was the Word: and the Word was with God: and the Word was God."

"That's the first part of St John's Gospel," said Sam, beginning to get excited. "Your little fragment came from a bible."

"More likely a gospel book, or a single copy of one gospel for the abbey's use," corrected Niall. "It was rare even for a very rich monastery to possess a copy of the whole Bible bound together. Let's not forget that this is one fragment of one page. But what a page. It could hardly be more exciting." Niall grabbed his cold coffee and drained it in one swig, then leapt to his feet. "Come on, then," he cried. Then he paused and looked at Bry. "Is there more?" he asked.

"A little. As you know, we can't do chemical tests for date, or to confirm the constituents of the ink, for fear of destroying the piece altogether, but after our last talk I took forward your proposal regarding preservation, and we have treated the back surface of the fragment with a glycerol solution. This softened and stabilised the fabric sufficiently that we were able to flatten it out slightly, and we were able to remove a small amount of sooty residue from the ventral surface. The result, as you've seen, is that some of the markings have become visible in normal daylight, and we are now able to see evidence of colour."

"Oak gall ink, fine vellum, colour and the first lines of a gospel…" said Niall, teasingly.

"First page of an illuminated manuscript," said Sam.

"Yes, I think so. All the evidence you've brought to light supports the idea that the fragment dates back to monastic times, and I'm very happy to be able to tell you…" Niall reached into his breast pocket and pulled out an envelope, which he began waving about excitedly, "carbon dating results on the hand give us a date of 1200 ± 50 BP."

Sam whooped but I was none the wiser. "One thousand two hundred years before present," said Niall. "Roughly 800AD, which puts it right at the point where monasteries were being sacked all over Celtic Christendom."

Bry jumped up and high fived Sam and the three of them began to do a daft dance around the table. The couple at the next table looked on disapprovingly and muttered to each other. I hid behind my latte and thanked my lucky stars we were in London, where nobody knows anybody else.

The drive home was as nightmarish as expected. Niall drove first, and I lay down on the back seat and tried not to feel sick. The plan was that he would drive until we passed Birmingham, or until he started to feel too tired to concentrate, whichever came first, but as it was we didn't even reach Birmingham. Somewhere north of Oxford we came to a grinding halt as the motorway shut down completely. Eventually, traffic news on the radio told us there was a jack-knifed lorry in the carriageway ahead of us and the motorway would be closed for some time. Sam got out and stretched his legs in the middle of the fast lane while Niall got on the phone to John.

"Sorry, mate." he said. "Major traffic disruption on the M40. You'd better go to plan B, in case we don't get through."

He listened for a while, nodding, but signed off without saying anything more than "Thanks, John, I owe you." Then he flopped back into the car and rested his head on the back of the seat. "I need to close my eyes for a minute," he mumbled.

"Swap now," I suggested. "Get some shut-eye in the back seat and Sam can keep me company. This lot isn't going to move any time soon, anyway."

No sooner said than done. Niall slept for four hours while Sam and I bored one another to death with I-spy and twenty questions. Eventually the traffic started to move with glacial slowness, but by that time it was after six and there were more reports of major bottlenecks north of Birmingham. I pulled off at the first motorway services we came to, and Niall managed to get the last room available in the hotel. The three of us had to share a family room (Sam hid in the car while we booked, so they wouldn't notice he was clearly over the 15 years age limit for sharing a family room).

There was a bit of adolescent hilarity over who was to sleep on the trundle bed and who would take the double bed, but Niall sorted that out by announcing that Sam would take the trundle and he would sleep on the sofa. "I need your Mum to drive tomorrow," he pointed out, "and she hasn't had a proper sleep yet."

Sam subsided without fuss, and I think we all got some sleep. We started out early the next day and passed Birmingham just as the morning rush was beginning. From there it was plain sailing all the way to Oban, with only a brief slow-down as we passed through the centre of Glasgow. I don't think I've ever been so pleased to see the dear old Calmac terminal.

18

Most of the team were crowded together upstairs in a corner of the passenger lounge. John and his students had closed down the dig and were ready to head back to Nottingham to start writing up their notes. John looked tanned and relaxed, and declared himself ready for a fresh onslaught of first year students, if he could just manage a couple of weeks to get the paperwork out of the way.

Lisbet and Ree were arm-in-arm on one chair, sharing a mobile phone as they chatted in turn to friends they hadn't seen for weeks. Louise, Rick and Amanda were slumped in a corner looking bored, while Lily was deep in holiday reading. Tim and Annette had already departed, as they were both booked into the same conference in the Middle East and had to catch a plane. As we walked into the terminal, John already had his hand out for his winnings. Niall grinned at him as he handed it over, saying that the discoveries they'd made had been worth every penny.

I planned to board the mid-afternoon ferry to Mull – back to my newly-repaired roof and empty rooms. Niall and Sam were saying their goodbyes too. Niall had work to catch up on in the Oban office of AIAS, and would meet up with John and Tim for a formal post-mortem of the dig. Sam's plan was to travel over to Mull with me, and in a couple of weeks make his way to freshers' week at university. He has matured so much this year. It's hard to keep in mind that he's only just beginning his tertiary studies. I hope uni lives up to his expectations after the excitement of the last two summers.

I wondered how he and Niall would manage their relationship, being separated so much of the time. Still, the depth of commitment they'd shown for each other over the last few weeks didn't arise fully formed out of nothing. I guessed they must have known before the beginning of this summer that they wanted to be together, which suggests they were running a long-distance relationship while Sam was still in his last year at boarding school. In other words, during the time I'd innocently reassured myself that, having been burnt once, Sam would take some time before getting involved with anyone else. It goes to show how little mothers know about their sons.

Big John had already talked his team through the dig and confirmed the progress they had all made, as they were preparing to leave Lismore this morning, but before we parted for the last time Niall wanted to share the London news with them. Sam leaned his head on Niall's shoulder and we all crowded round the screen of his laptop as it slowly began to show a blurred image.

I moved back a little to let the students in. After all, I'd already seen it. A moment later the image sharpened and the surface of a piece of vellum took shape. On it, some darker lines hinted at pattern. We all stared, willing the lines to make sense. At top left on the screen was the largest shape, a thickened line with a slight curve to it, and another thick line crossed it at the top. Other lines were thinner and fainter. I blinked and rubbed my eyes. I still found it hard to make sense of what I saw, but John, Ree and Lisbet all nodded at one another. It clearly meant something to them. Niall looked round at his audience.

"Not the Life of Moluag," he said, "but this looks to me very like a fragment of one of the gospels. Look here," he gestured toward the largest shape and its associated faint lines. "Note the capital, or majuscule, 'I'. Most of the colour on the fragment is associated with this letter. Here, this little curved bit, may be a 'p'. And below it, the downward pointing triangle: probably a 'v'." He tilted the screen, trying to show them a better view. I smothered a snort – I've done exactly the same thing with a mobile phone. Intuitively, you treat it as you would a three-dimensional view: twisting the picture, or tilting your head, trying vainly to get a different viewpoint. Niall shrugged, and smiled up at the circle of surrounding faces.

"In principio erat Verbum," he said.

"Yes!" The shout went up from Lisbet, and then they were all pounding one another on the back.

"I believe we now have proof there was at least one high quality book present on Lismore at the beginning of the ninth century. We have more than just the words to support that conjecture. The letters we've been able to make out are clearly written in the style called 'Insular Majuscule'."

Niall paused and looked round at us. "Time for a lecture, boys and girls," he said. "Make yourselves comfortable."

Ree and Lisbet subsided happily into one chair together, and the rest gathered round, perching on chair arms, or leaning over their backs. This was clearly something they were used to.

"The history of Insular script is quite interesting. In around the fourth century A.D. scribes and scholars in Europe began writing in a script called half-uncial, derived from Roman cursive minuscule. The Roman script was quite angular, suitable for writing on rough surfaces like papyrus, but the development of smoother writing surfaces such as parchment and vellum allowed for the creation of a rounded script that is much easier to read, and probably more comfortable to write.

"In Ireland and mainland Britain, half-uncial gradually become rounder and more embellished until it reached its final form, insular majuscule. This was the script used in famous surviving works such as the Lindisfarne Gospels, and the Book of Kells with its wonderful illuminated capitals. Even with only a handful of letters surviving on our scrap of vellum, we can clearly see evidence of the Insular style. As you know, those famous works are extensively and beautifully illuminated, and we have evidence of colour associated with our capital I."

Niall flicked through the images on the screen until the one with the clearest image of the writing was showing.

"Dr Desart and his team identified that the main ink used

in the piece is very high in iron, and is most likely oak gall ink. The Book of Kells was written in oak gall ink, and recipes for it have survived in monastic records. All of this is clear evidence of a monastic association for the site at Annaid. It expands our understanding of the monastic community on Lismore to a whole new area of the island.

"It would beggar belief for the handless skeleton at Achnacroish not to relate to our discovery at Annaid. Two of the skeletons, including the mutilated one, date to around the end of the eighth century, and therefore they fit with the era of Viking incursions. However, the first skeleton we found, the one with the prayer stone, must have been reburied at that time. His dates show that he lived in the early seventh century, and so could be associated with the founding of the monastic tradition here on Lismore.

"It can't be Moluag himself – we know he died at Rosemarkie, on the Black Isle, and his grave site was marked with a Pictish symbol stone – but the early date for our first skeleton, with its associated prayer stone, links the later burials to the seventh century, less than a century after Moluag is said to have founded Lismore."

Niall looked up at his audience again. "Precis, please?" he asked them.

Sam was game. "You're saying that we've demonstrated a link between early years of the monastic tradition at Achnacroish and the kist you discovered at Annaid, even though the contents of the kist date from two hundred years later."

Niall smiled at him. "Absolutely right. What we have is a veritable cairn of white pebbles, the socket for a stone cross or pillar, and an array of adult burials, one buried with a Christian symbol. I think we can claim conclusively to have found the site of a monastery which lasted several hundred years, and I believe we can make a good case that the Annaid find is related, which enables us to demonstrate monastic activity right down to the south coast of Lismore.

"By the time these results are written up, we'll have expanded our understanding of the life and times of Moluag immensely. He'll never be as famous as St Columba, and his monastic foundation disappeared where Iona survived, but our work will help to ensure that he isn't forgotten."

"So do you still think it can't be part of a bible?" I asked.

"Yes I do. Very few whole bibles were produced before the era of printing, even in monasteries, but gospel books were produced for private study, and for ceremonial purposes. Gospel books were the most common form of illuminated manuscript until about the end of the tenth century, when bibles and psalters became more common. A psalter is a book of the psalms, sometimes with musical notation," Niall added.

Lisbet and Ree had been holding a whispered conference. "What about the Book of Deer?" they asked. "Could our one have been like that?"

"Good question." Niall looked around once more at the circle of faces. "What is the Book of Deer? Anyone?"

There was a moment's pause, then Rick spoke up. "It's a gospel book too. Thought to have been made in Scotland during the tenth century. I don't know much about it, though."

"Thanks, Rick. Anyone else?"

I looked at the serious, focused faces around me and realised that our shared conference about the vellum scrap had turned into an impromptu seminar. A look of fierce concentration was fixed on Ree's face. "It's probably not helpful," she said, "but I thought the most famous thing about the Book of Deer was that part of it was written in true Scots Gaelic. But wouldn't that make it later than the tenth century?"

"Correct." Niall gave her a pleased nod. "In fact, the only extant copy of the Book of Deer, currently held in the Cambridge University Library is a copy of the tenth century manuscript, which is now lost. The twelfth century copy faithfully reproduces the original text, but there are also a series of hand-written glosses in Scots Gaelic. It's the first recorded instance of written Gaelic in Scotland. All previous fragments had been written in Irish Gaelic. That is its primary claim to fame, although the book itself is beautifully made and would still be a precious artefact in its own right, even without the later additions."

He paused and I got in with my question. "You said it was made in Scotland, although it has ended up in Cambridge. Are you saying it might have come from Lismore?"

"No, sadly not. There's good evidence to suggest that the copy was made at the monastery of Old Deer in Aberdeenshire. Very likely the original was also created there. In a sense that makes the book even more intriguing for scholars, because the area was the heartland of a Pictish community. Although by the twelfth century the Picts were no more, and there's no suggestion of any Pictish writing in the Book, the glosses do discuss the history of kings and the politics of the area, and they give us a great insight into a part of our history that is otherwise very poorly attested.

"Now, there are two reasons I don't think our fragment belonged to a gospel book like the Book of Deer. Would anyone like to hazard a guess as to what those are?"

We all looked at one another, but no-one could think of anything to add.

"Okay. What size is the Book of Deer?"

"Oh." Lisbet grabbed his attention. "It's really small."

"That's right. It's no bigger than a modern paperback book. It was designed for personal use, not for display to a congregation. Here, take a look at this…"

Niall opened up the laptop again and displayed the best infrared picture of the Lismore fragment. He pulled the window to one side of the screen and opened another to the Book of Deer website. Finding a picture of one of the pages, he snapped it up to the first window so that the two pictures sat side by side. Then he adjusted the zoom on the Lismore fragment. "I've set them both to about the same level of magnification," he said. "What do you see?"

"The text on our fragment is much bigger," observed Sam.

"Yes. In order to fit four gospels into a little, hand-held

book the scribe had to use quite small writing. You can see, too, that the script is more angular than ours. It's been written in a script called Irish minuscule, and although there is slight ornamentation around the capitals, there's no colour or complex illumination.

"The gospel book of Saint Cuthbert, which is held in the British Library, is another small personal volume. It was written in insular majuscule; the letters are rounder and slightly larger than the script in the Book of Deer, but there was still minimal use of ornamentation or colour. The beautifully crafted famous books, like the Book of Kells, were made to be seen as much as read. I don't think we have anything quite so elaborate here, although of course it's difficult to extrapolate from such a small sample, but our scrap undoubtedly belonged to a larger book than either the Book of Deer or the Saint Cuthbert Gospel.

"Both the size and the style of the letters on our scrap of vellum suggest they were intended to be part of an illustrated page. And the few letters we have are definitely insular majuscule, which supports the idea that it was part of a larger volume, intended to be shared. 'In the beginning was the Word' is the starting text of John, and it may have been that our injured monk was working on a new illuminated manuscript when he was attacked. Alternatively, he could have been protecting one of the monastery's precious books."

There was a dreamy look on Niall's face. He stared off across the terminal lounge and out through its glass wall to the harbour beyond, but it wasn't hard to guess that his thoughts were back there, on Lismore.

"I wonder if his hand was severed down at Annaid, and the body brought back here to the monastery. I can't think of any reason that a monk injured in the monastery precincts would have part of his anatomy taken to Annaid to be buried."

"Perhaps he was a hermit," I suggested. "Maybe he was working away on a new manuscript in the peace and quiet of Annaid when raiders arrived."

"Now, there's a thought." Niall was getting excited. Sam gave him room to move as he began to wave his arms about. "A hermit's scriptorium; a peaceful place to work, away from the bustle of the main monastic site. A hermit, or a small community of scribes working on a special project. The date range we have for the hand puts it right at the time of Norse raiders – 800 A.D. plus or minus a few decades. Perhaps our man was trying to protect the manuscript, and they had to cut off his hand to force him to relinquish the valuable artefact.

"Later, the surviving monks, or those from the monastery, could have found him and taken him back to Port Moluag. He certainly lived long enough for the injury to begin to heal. Perhaps the hand was rescued from the ruins of a burnt building, or maybe it was found later. Either way, it was treated with great respect: laid in that stone reliquary, which was then carefully placed in what might have been the very building in which he fell, protecting the object he must have felt was the most precious thing in the world."

"The Book of Lismore," I said.

"Funny you should say that," said Niall. "There is a real Book of Lismore, sometimes also called the Book of the Dean of Lismore, containing collections of Gaelic tales and histories, which was published in the sixteenth century. There are also rumours about a Great Book of Lismore, a Bible or Gospel book dating to the time that Lismore was the centre of its own diocese, and the church at Port Moluag was the Cathedral of the Isles, or perhaps even earlier to the height of the monastic period.

"Many people think the Great Book of Lismore refers to the diocese of Lismore in Ireland, and has nothing to do with the Scottish island. There is a well-founded theory, however, that the Book of Kells was begun on Iona, by Columba's monastic foundation, and it only moved to Kells in Ireland when the Vikings began raiding regularly and much of the abbey and its surroundings were pillaged. Perhaps we could argue for the Book of Lismore originating here in the same way."

"Whatever our man was holding, I wonder if the raiders actually took the book," said Sam. "Or did the dead hand hold it so tightly that they were forced to leave without it? I can't see the Vikings being put off by such a grisly trophy, though. They didn't seem to mind any amount of bloodshed and mutilation, so long as they were the ones who were handing it out."

"That's a nice thought, though." Niall still had an abstracted expression on his face as he gazed into the distance, as if seeing the peaceful landscape at Annaid with its quiet, family-sized harbour and home fields, and the little cell set back into the cliff-side, overlooking the sea. A small, homely scene desecrated in a moment by an invasion of violent men: blood spilt, sacrilege done. A brave man, trying to protect the one thing that meant more to him than his own life. Had he succeeded? Had his determination to keep hold of the manuscript, even after death, been sufficient to frighten off the raiders? Or perhaps cause them to admire the bravery of a man who could have had no physical defence against them?

I imagined the raiders departing, leaving the dead behind them, taking only what was valuable to them, leaving a blood-stained book in a burning building. Hard to imagine they would have got much of value from such a pocket-sized landscape: perhaps some food supplies, a goat or a cow, a slave or two if the violence had been restrained. Although the severed hand argued against restraint.

Perhaps brethren from the monastery, coming upon the scene later, anticipating only sorrow and finding it in full measure, also found it alleviated by the presence of a sacred work, a corner of the manuscript still firmly held in the grasp of a dead hand. An image of that dead hand, sealed in its box, made its way into my mind. I still felt a brief shiver of revulsion, but my attitude to it was changing now that it was beginning to have its own story.

I pictured the monks raising the injured man and bearing him away with reverence. Taking the precious manuscript back to the monastery, for what little safety it might find there against the next raid, or the next. It was very easy to imagine them cleansing the desecrated place, and then leaving something holy and sanctified to watch over the hermitage, even though its saint was dead.

In my mind's eye, I watched them carefully separate the dead hand from the book, leaving in its grip a small piece of the sacred work it protected, before wrapping the precious relic in finest linen and making a box for it: a reliquary, to hold the essence of the saint as he watched over Annaid for all eternity.

"We'll never know," said Niall, laying his hand on Sam's shoulder. Sam's hand came up and covered it and we all stood in silence for a moment. "We can find out a lot, we diggers-up of the past, but we can't really know what happened."

19

It was lovely to have Sam home again. I made the most of our precious few days of holiday. We went for long walks together, and I showed him all my favourite haunts. We slept in, and breakfasted in our pyjamas on pancakes, or bacon sandwiches. We stayed up late into the night, playing board games, and computer games, and always talking.

At first we were a little hesitant with each other. Niall was the elephant in the room – the unspoken subtext to our daily conversations. Soon enough, though, the talk flowed freely between us, and I indulged myself in animated arguments with him about life, the world, the state of politics, whatever caught our interest. It was like having another adult in the house.

That thought was sobering. It was exactly like having another adult in the house. Sam was truly adult now, despite his sometimes half-baked and poorly constructed arguments. Having these conversations with my son made me realise how dysfunctional my relationship with my husband had been. I thought back to the beginnings of my marriage to Drew and mentally worked my way forward, wincing through the memory of arguments, attacks, and constant derision and insult. I couldn't remember that we'd ever engaged in mutually respectful adult conversation. How sad.

We went back to Calgary Bay and walked the crescent of white sand along and back again, sharing a new reminiscence – our first proper day spent with Niall. With his hands in his pockets, Sam strolled beside me, looking relaxed and happy, a sweet smile creasing his face again and again as he talked about the man he loved. It was love. I wasn't in any doubt about that. I hoped Niall Webster knew exactly what he'd got in Sam Longmore, and appreciated it properly.

It wasn't a peaceful walk. The campsite was full of caravans and rough campers, packed in cheek by jowl, and the sand was dotted with families enjoying the rarity of a hot, dry day on Mull. I couldn't help but compare this lovely summer day with the cool, windy, lonely day when the Calgary Chess Queen came into my life. Calgary Bay has many aspects, and they are all beautiful. Even as the evening wore on, and those with small children headed off to dinner, bath and bed, there were still people arriving – young adults and older couples, settling in for the long Scottish summer evening.

Fire were lit, and bottles opened, and soon the sound of a guitar drifted over the machair, accompanied by a lone voice singing.

Sam had rolled up his trousers and was trudging shin-deep through the shushing waves. He stopped for a moment and stared at his feet, shading his eyes from the light bouncing off the surface of the sea.

"Mum, come and look at this."

I shucked off my sandals and joined him in the water. It was pleasantly cool after the heat of the sand, and a layer of foam on the wave crests stroked my legs as it passed. I looked where Sam was looking.

There in the water, not two feet from his legs, a huge shoal of tiny fish was swimming. They darted and gleamed in the shadows, moving as one across the rippled sea floor. My balance wobbled and my foot moved, enough to startle them, and the whole school dashed for the safety of deeper water. Behind them a flat fish moved, shucking a wake of sand behind it, and sank back into invisibility a few feet away.

I stood up and stared out to sea, holding my hand up to ward off the glare of the setting sun. The sky was a watercolour, and the sun painted a glorious golden pathway across the water, pointing straight at the horizon. I sighed in pure contentment.

"It's lovely tonight, isn't it, Mum?" Sam waded out of the water and picked up his shoes and socks. "Every time I come here I'm surprised again by how beautiful it is." He shuffled up the beach, grinding his feet into the soft sand, and I followed him with my sandals dangling from one hand. "I wish there was somewhere like this near Montrose."

There we have it. Notice served that I need to prepare for the end of this idyll. Sam's mind was clearly on his upcoming first semester at uni, and for all that I was going to miss him I was glad to see him looking forward. I wondered when he would go.

"I'm thinking of going tomorrow," he said, as if he'd read my mind. "Niall has the weekend free, and he's going to run me over, help me settle in. You don't mind, do you, Mum?"

Bit late to ask that, I thought. I'd been looking forward to driving across the mainland, seeing where Sam would be studying and making sure he was all set. I smiled and told him it was fine. It was the truth. I had a feeling Sam was going to be just fine.

"I'll see you soon," he said as we pulled out of the car park. "Niall has something to do at Annaid. He wants to take us back there in a few weeks. We'll pick you up in the RIB. He's going to let me know when."

I glanced across at him, but his face gave nothing away. I wondered what Niall had in mind, but I didn't ask. Let them enjoy their secret.

"You can come, can't you, Mum?"

"I'm sure I can," I said. "Just let me know the time and place and I'll make sure I'm there."

The sun's rays shot straight through the rear windscreen as I headed the car away from the beach, dazzling me with their reflection in the rear-view mirror. I looked back as we turned away, and the slow, late fall of dusk turned the water into a sheet of silver, and the dancing, firelit figures on the sand into creatures out of legend. Calgary Bay was showing another of its magical faces.

20

At first I thought the wind was getting up, but the noise came again – a faint knock at the door, and a rattle of the latch. Who could it be at this hour?

As I walked through the darkened kitchen I thought I could see a figure, standing at the corner of the porch. Someone tall – male – my heart lurched. What if it was Drew? I told myself to get a grip; Drew would have walked straight in and attempted to dominate the proceedings. He might have knocked, but he would never have waited. It couldn't be Sam. I'd seen him safe onto the ferry earlier in the afternoon, off to his induction week at uni. He'd arranged to meet Niall in Oban. It was a last chance for them to spend some quality time together before the term started in earnest.

It was Ewan. As I opened the door a squally wind blew across the garden and the aroma of whisky gusted into the house. Ewan straightened up from where he'd been leaning on the porch wall. He folded his arms and attempted to look sober. I stepped back and gestured him through to the kitchen. He wavered slightly as he passed me, and put out one arm to brace himself against the wall. The length of him came up against me, and I leaned into his warmth for a moment, but he recovered himself and moved on.

By the time I got back inside he was in the kitchen, making tea for us both. I winced as the spout of the kettle rattled against the edge of his mug, but he finished the process unscathed and we repaired to the living room. I curled myself up on the larger of my two armchairs, while Ewan made himself comfortable on the couch. He set his mug down on the coffee table and sat back, stretching his long legs out in front of him. He closed his eyes and visibly relaxed.

I held my mug up in front of me like a talisman and observed him through the steam. Those long, long legs, strong hands, the lean strength of him in jeans and faded shirt. I remembered the curve of his ribs under my fingers, the pulse point in the hollow of his throat, the heat of his skin, his weight on me. For a moment I closed my own eyes, and my hand shook.

When I opened them he was looking at me.

"I wanted…" he said. He lowered his gaze and swallowed, obviously uncomfortable. He rummaged in the pockets of his jacket and pulled out his hip flask. Uncapping it, he waved it invitingly towards me. I shook my head, and he decanted a generous slug into his tea. The sweet, smoky aroma of the alcohol reached me and for a moment I was tempted to join him. Still, I'd learned through bitter experience to be very wary of men who drink, and I needed to keep all my wits about me in case this man, whom I wanted very much to keep on trusting, turned out to be as dangerous as the one I once called my husband.

"I wanted to talk to you. We never seem to find the time."

I stared at him. I've lost count of the number of occasions when I've visited Hector to find Ewan unaccountably missing, or about to leave: even, once, in the process of opening the back door as I came in the front. I'd formed the unmistakeable impression that he was avoiding me.

"How's your Dad?" I asked him.

"He's fine. Old Matt came round this morning – his bitch has had puppies and he's looking for a home for one of the dogs. Dad's holding out. He says he doesn't want another dog, but I think he'll change his mind in time. What about you? Did you have any more trouble with your ex-husband?"

I thought back over the events of the last few weeks: Sam's kidnap and escape, and the revelation of his relationship with Niall. It all seemed so complicated. No doubt the time would come when I'd find myself telling Ewan all about it, and Bernie was still waiting for me to spill the beans, but I didn't want to go into all that now. Ewan was here for a reason – it had clearly taken quite a lot of alcohol to get him to the point of approaching me – and I wanted to find out what it was.

I crossed the room and sat on the sofa next to him, curling my feet up under myself so as not to touch him. He raised his mug to mine and I smiled at him. He took a gulp and set the mug down again. This time when he leaned back and closed his eyes, he put out his hand and took mine. I held myself still, hardly daring to breathe, feeling as though some wild creature had unaccountably come close, and wanting to make sure I didn't do anything that might frighten it away. He kept his eyes closed as he began to talk.

"There was this girl came here, when I was young. A summer visitor."

I nodded, though he couldn't see the gesture. Hector had talked about the travellers who came in the summer, selling goods, or skills such as tinkering, or sometimes just their labour. He'd talked about a traveller girl he spent time with, in the golden summer of his youth. He had his first kiss with his 'dark-haired lass', and paid for it in bruises when the girl's father came across the pair and beat them both with his belt.

Hector had taken his humiliation home to his father, expecting sympathy, and got the belt a second time for 'shaming our family.' The old man explained that traveller girls were not supposed to have anything to do with the local folk – her punishment may have been even more severe than his – and the boys were all warned to keep away from them, they were more trouble than they were worth.

But Ewan wasn't talking about travellers. "She was from the continent. French, or Belgian, I'm not sure which. These days it's common enough for tourists to come in from Europe and work for the season, but back then it was very unusual.

"She worked up at the manse. I suppose she was what city folk called an au pair. Kept an eye on the kids, did a bit of housework. She was supposed to teach the children

French, but she never got far with that.

"All us boys used to watch her. She was pretty – long, brown hair tied up on top of her head, big brown eyes, and lips we dreamed about kissing. I was already on the boats, away for days on end at sea. I used to torment myself with thoughts of one of the MacArthur boys getting his paws on her – them with their clean, soft hands from working in the shop." A look of contempt flickered briefly across his face.

"Sometimes I used to lie in my bunk and think on what her white skin must look like under her clothes. She dressed very modestly – more so than most of the local girls – a glimpse of legs under her skirts, and her cardigan pulled round her shoulders. Very prim and proper for the minister. Ha."

He laughed to himself, and his thumb moved over my wrist, stroking it. A ripple of pleasure shimmered through me, but I suppressed it. Something told me this tale was not the prelude to seduction.

"I thought I was the luckiest boy alive when I met her, coming home late from the town. It was the first day of a week's leave from the fishing, and I'd been in to pick up some shopping for the old man and meet the boys at the pub. I wasn't drunk," he opened one eye and gazed at me for a moment, gauging my response. "I'd had enough to be warm and comfortable. There'd been a song or two at the Arms, and I was humming one as I marched along. Coming abreast of the last house, there she was, and she fell into step with me. 'Going my way?' I asked her, and she smiled the enigmatic smile that drove us all wild.

"She'd made up her mind at last – and it was me she chose. I thought I'd died and gone to heaven that night. I'd never known a girl who could kiss like her, and one thing led to another on that walk home, laughing and teasing each other, tangling together and pulling apart, her flirting with me in the darkness, and then coming in close so I could take her in my arms and feel all of her, warm and ready for me. I suppose I should have seen sense when she pulled me into the abandoned croft and I found she had a blanket laid out, waiting for us. But I was beyond sense by that stage."

Intentionally or not, Ewan's story couldn't help but remind me of our own lovemaking last summer. I squirmed involuntarily, shifting my position on the sofa, and he let go of my hand. I wrapped it around my mug again, missing the warmth of his touch, as he carried on speaking.

"She kept me with her all that week. In daylight we both had our tasks, and if I saw her passing by on the road with her basket, or a handful of children at foot, our glances met and we pretended not to notice one another. But come the fall of darkness, there we were again, exploring everything we had to teach one another. Don't get me wrong – I knew fine she was no virgin – but there still seemed a freshness to her, as if the pleasure we discovered together was something new for her too. It was certainly a real eye-opener to me."

Ewan took another pull from his hip flask. It seemed to me that he'd probably had enough, but I was transfixed by the story he was telling me. This was the longest conversation I'd ever had out of him, although it was hardly a conversation, my contribution consisting of no more than an unseen nod and some encouraging noises. He might as well have been talking to himself.

"The summer wore down to its end, and I begrudged every moment I spent on the boats. Every couple of weeks I'd come up the hill with my pay in my pocket, clean and shave myself, and don my best clothes to court her all over again. She was very patient with my working lifestyle. She never complained about the times when I wasn't there.

"Come the early days of autumn, I went up to the manse to call on her, trousers pressed, clean handkerchief, a posy of wildflowers in my hand. I had the idea that I needed to get our relationship out in the open, to be able to see her in daylight without folks talking behind our backs.

"The minister's wife opened the door: a small woman who had the knack of blending into the background. To this day I can't remember her name. She looked me up and down and her mouth opened, though she didn't speak. She took in my slicked-back hair and handful of blooms and smiled, a look of pity. 'She's gone,' she said. 'Away the first boat. Minister drove her down there.'

"I dragged myself home, heels scuffing in the dust of the road. The flowers I threw in the ditch. For the rest of my week's leave I sat at home. I was in no mood to socialise, and no-one came to call on me. It's good company you get at the bar, but they're equally good company to all comers, so long as there's beer in the tap and whisky on the shelf. They didn't miss me."

I put out a hand and laid it on his arm, intending to offer comfort, but he flinched away from the touch, although his voice remained light.

"It was a long stint on the boats, the last one of the year. I promised my father I wouldn't go out on the winter trawls. It was too dangerous. This time when I signed off there was no pretty girl waiting for me on the trudge home. I dumped my bag and went down to the town, looking to drown my sorrows. The place was in a welter of speculation, the bar abuzz with the gossip. That was when I found out what she'd been up to, all those times I was away at sea.

"The MacArthur boys – both the brothers – had been up at the doctor with the pox. Gonorrhoea. These days it's not the life sentence it used to be – modern antibiotics see it off pretty quick, once you know what you've got – but their reputation was shot. No-one looks twice at a man who tumbles a pretty girl. If she doesn't have the sense to say no, what blame is there to him? It was considered to be normal for a man to have his needs met, one way or another. But to sleep with a dirty girl –both of them, at the same time, or so people were saying, and more of the same. Did they share her round, time and about? Or did the three of them do it together? There was plenty more talk like that. You'd think, to hear the gossip, that everyone had seen through her, bar those two foolish boys."

Ewan glanced at me. His face wore a self-deprecating smile. He looked as though he'd told this story before, and knew the effect it would have on his listeners. I could imagine him telling it down the pub in later years, once the gossips had stopped talking. I couldn't understand why he thought the story would concern me. I had a child – it was pretty clear I'd had a sex life, and I didn't expect him to be any different. He looked down at his hands before continuing.

"A girl like that? Well, she was gone, there was no saving her reputation. Anything could be said, and was. It was just as well she hadn't drawn anyone else into her clutches, that was all the good that people could say for her. I kept my head down – I didn't think it was my imagination that some looked askance at me when they spoke about her. My visit to the manse had not gone unnoticed.

"A few days later I confided in my Dad. I had to. I was experiencing some symptoms myself, and I didn't dare go to the surgery. A healthy young man like me? What business could I have with the doctor? No, the boys would have guessed soon enough what it was about.

"Dad took himself in, and invited old Doctor MacIlroy to taste his new brew. A few nights later he called by, and once the two of them were warmed through by a good dram, Dad called me in and told the Doctor what was what. He looked me over – took some blood – gave me a solid lecture about taking precautions, but to my relief not one about my incontinent behaviour. I didn't need anyone to tell me how stupid I'd been."

Ewan jumped up and headed towards the kitchen. He paused when he got to the doorway and leaned against the wall to steady himself, then turned and walked back to me. He refused to meet my eye as he sat down again. I held my hands in my lap to stop myself from touching him and tried to think of something supportive to say. I thought I knew what was coming next, though I was only partly right.

"I had it too – gonorrhoea. She'd given me something else as well. A little parting gift I think the MacArthur boys had avoided. Herpes. It's more common these days. They say that up to half of all sexually active adults are infected, and there are good antiviral treatments now. But not in those days.

"I'd never heard of it before, and I'd listened to many a gory tale on the boats about the dangers posed by sex. Most people who've had it don't even know they've been exposed – at worst, they feel like they've had a bad dose of the flu and then it's all over – but a few people get regular recurrences."

He stood again, unable to keep still, and walked up and down in front of me.

"In the beginning there was no treatment, nothing that could be done. Every few weeks or so I'd get a sharp pain in my genitals, then the blisters would come up, hot like the aftermath of burns. In a few days they burst, then the pain is raw and harsh until the skin heals over and there's relief. Until the next time. I'm on anti-virals now. They prevent most outbreaks, but I can't ever be completely sure I'm free of it."

He stopped pacing and turned his eyes onto my face. The double frown-line between his brows stood out deep and clear, and as I met his gaze he winced and looked away. He threw himself down on the sofa again and leaned forward, his head between his hands. His voice reached me, muffled but clear. "I made you have sex with me and I knew I shouldn't do it. I was careful. You saw me take precautions. But I shouldn't have done it."

He ground his palms into his eye sockets and growled in frustration. Then he looked across at me, eyes red and filled with a despairing expression. "I should have left you alone."

I put my hands on his arm, solid with corded muscle, and leaned on it comfortingly. "I wanted it too," I said. "I wanted you so much. I chose to take the risk."

"No, you didn't. You didn't know what risk you were taking."

I couldn't argue with that. I took an unknown risk, but if you'd asked me I'd have said Ewan was as safe as houses. I'd never known him to be in any kind of relationship. He seemed safe because he was such a loner. I suppose if I thought about it at all, I'd have guessed that by sleeping with me he was breaking the habit of years. He seemed as celibate as a monk. As it appears he truly was – though not for any reason I might have imagined.

"Ewan, is this why you don't want a relationship with me? Because you're worried you might pass it on?" He didn't answer. "We can work with this. You said it yourself – there are treatments these days – and there are safe methods we can use. It doesn't have to mean you can never have a relationship."

He shook his head savagely, and gripped my hands in his own. I winced and looked down at my knuckles, white in the strength of his grasp, willing myself not to pull away.

"After I slept with you, I had the worst attack in over a decade. Even the anti-virals only suppress the thing. There's no cure for it. I learned in my twenties that if I had sex, I would stir it up again. It wants me to pass it on."

"It's only a virus," I said, surreptitiously trying to draw my hands out of his grip. "It doesn't have a mind of its own."

He laughed, an explosive sound not far removed from a cry. "It might as well have. I know from bitter experience what will happen if I allow myself to have a sex life." He let go suddenly and pulled away, throwing himself against the sofa back and closing his eyes again. "I can't be what you want, Cas. I don't want to. The price is too high."

This time when he pulled the hip flask from his pocket, I held my hand out for my own share. The liquor went down hard and burned its way down my gullet all the way to my stomach, where it sat like a small unexploded bomb. I took a second swig and let it trickle slowly down my throat while I thought ferociously.

He was right, of course. I couldn't ask him to do something with me that, no matter how pleasurable, had such horrible consequences for him. And to be honest, I wasn't at all sure I wanted to take the risk of catching it. I told myself I appreciated his honesty – imagine if he hadn't told me, and then I found out I'd got it – but I couldn't help but feel cheated. This lovely man, who became a friend long before he was briefly my lover. It wasn't fair.

By the time we finished off the whisky I was half asleep myself, and Ewan had passed beyond drunk into a kind of alcohol-induced trance. I leaned back into the cushions as he gently toppled over sideways, coming to rest with his head in my lap. I stroked his hair and tried to ignore my spinning head as he sank into sleep.

I must have dozed off myself, because I came awake in the dark to find that he'd rolled over. Head still resting on my lap, he pressed his nose into my crotch and rubbed it against me. A powerful jolt of arousal rocked through me as he made noises, not so much snoring as rumbling deep in his throat. Wherever he was in his whisky-soaked dreams, it was clearly a very nice place to be, but the rise of pleasure died in the realisation of our mutual plight. Apparently we wanted each other, but the consequence of that desire would be pain for him and incalculable risk for me.

The alcohol in my gut seemed to have turned to ice, and I felt a hard lump of unshed tears in my throat. I wondered if there could be any future for us, knowing what I now did. And I wondered how drunk Ewan really was, and quite what he would remember when he came round again.

The morning light found me still there, cradling his head in my hands. I rotated my neck slowly, wincing at its stiffness, before easing myself out from under and lowering his head to the cushions. I moved as quietly as I could, but as my hand touched the door handle I heard him groan and roll over. I looked back just as his eyes opened.

His face blanched as his gaze met mine, and I held up one hand, palm outward. "Nothing happened," I said. "We just talked." I tried not to feel humiliated by the expression of relief that flickered across his face. "I'll put the kettle on for some tea," I said, and turned away.

When he took his leave, a little later that morning, I got my answer, or at least part of it. I walked with him to the gate, not knowing how we would say goodbye to each other, or even if it was possible to openly acknowledge what we'd shared during the night. I put my hand out to stop him walking away, and passed over the hip flask that had ended up in my own pocket. He took it from me, his fingers warm on mine. For a moment, he met my eye and held my gaze.

I clutched at his arm, holding him back as he turned away. "Ewan," I pleaded. "We both took the risk. My husband slept with other women. Maybe I've already had herpes? I might even be immune."

He shook his head, but I persisted. "For all you know I might have given you something. You don't know, Ewan. There's no way of knowing. There's always a risk, but we'd be taking it together."

He jerked under my grip and I released him, spreading my fingers in a gesture of letting go. His eyes were kind, but distant – he'd already shut me out. He nodded in recognition of whatever unspoken thing lay behind my eyes. "You should get checked out," he said. "Just in case." His gaze fell, and he turned away, his last words almost lost in the movement. "I'm sorry."

***

Dr Parkinson was on duty. I was grateful it wasn't Dr Allinson. He's a good doctor, but I didn't feel like confiding in a man at the moment. Dr Parkinson was brusque and kind. She listened to my tale of woe, and asked me sensible if penetrating questions. I expected to feel humiliated at having to share private details of my sex life, but it was a relief to get all the worries out in the open. She took blood tests, and examined me physically, but explained that, as far as *Herpes simplex* was concerned, if I had no symptoms then I couldn't be tested. She would need live virus from an open blister to confirm infection.

She grilled me on my general health. How had I been since I slept with him? Had I experienced any illness, especially flu-like symptoms? When I told her that I felt better than I had in years, and my health was perfect, she told me not to worry. The chances I'd become a herpes carrier were slim-to-none, and I should put it out of my mind. I'd been lucky.

We talked about the characteristics of the disease. She confirmed that some people are particularly susceptible to the virus's action, and seem to have more frequent and more severe attacks than the norm. It might be that there are different forms of the virus, some more virulent than others. Equally, it could be that some people are more vulnerable to viral attack.

At the end of the appointment I stood, but she gestured me to sit again.

"You've been very careful not to share with me the name of your lover, and I, of course, cannot break patient confidentiality. However, I would like you and your friend to come and see me together. I probably cannot offer any new treatment, but there are things you can do – modifications of behaviour and expectation – to make sex between you possible, and to minimise the risk."

"I think…um." I paused for a moment to collect my thoughts, and make sure of what I was going to say. I met her sympathetic gaze. "He was drunk when he told me. I think he had to get drunk before he could tell me." She was nodding. "I don't think it will be good for us if I try to get him drunk again, and he's made it pretty clear he doesn't want to talk about it anymore. As far as he's concerned, it's over."

Tears stood in my eyes, but I didn't let them fall. Ewan was worth more than that. I'd already decided that friendship was more important than sex. I needed Ewan to believe me if our friendship was going to endure, but most of all I needed to convince myself.

I began to raise myself again, but Dr Parkinson put out one hand to stop me. She reached out the other and gently tugged aside the scarf around my neck. I flinched and closed my eyes, not wanting to see the expression in hers.

Gently she turned my head from side to side. I knew precisely what she was seeing: a faint line of bruises on the sides of my neck – and the thumbprints, now almost invisible in pastel shades, either side of my throat. I opened my eyes to find her regarding me steadily.

"That looks sore." I nodded. "Any difficulty in speaking?"

"At first, I guess. I didn't really talk to anyone for a few days. By then it had settled down a bit."

She held my eyes for a long moment. "Was it…?"

The expression on her face told me what she was thinking. "Oh, no. He never would. No – it was my ex-husband. He wanted me to do something and I refused. He doesn't like that."

"So I see." Her fingers were cool on my neck and shoulders, as she wrapped the scarf around me again. "Did you go to the police?"

"No. I don't see the point. They'll make the whole thing really difficult, and nothing will ever be done. It'll just make Drew angrier, and if he can't take it out on me then he'll turn on my son."

Dr Parkinson turned and wrote a brief remark in my notes. I was relieved to see nothing in her eyes but concern and compassion. She might disapprove of me keeping it to myself, but at least she didn't judge me for it.

"Cas, I would strongly advise you to report this. The evidence I see before me is very clear, and in my experience a person who has done this once will do so again and again. You say he's no longer your husband, and yet he still behaves this way. It's possible it will never stop, unless you take steps to deal with him. Were there any witnesses?"

"Only one." I swallowed harshly, biting back on the temptation to say his name. "My friend saw it. He took a picture on his phone before chasing my ex away."

"Then you have a good chance of a successful outcome. If you decide to report this, please do give my name to the police. I would be happy to give a statement about your injuries."

"Okay. Thank you." I pulled myself together and left. I was about ninety-nine percent sure I wasn't going to report Drew's assault. He came off very poorly – to have been seen off by his ex-wife and another man must have been mortifying. I was quite sure he was still seething over the humiliation, but somehow I felt the incident marked the true end of our relationship. I'd stood up to Drew and lived to tell the tale. I didn't think he'd be back.

21

I sat in the front of the RIB as Niall steered it onto the sand at Annaid's tiny beach. The tide was out and we picked our way across shingle-strewn sand to the high tide mark. Sam and Niall dragged the boat behind us and lashed its mooring rope to a spindly rowan that leaned over the bay. I lugged the picnic bags up the beach and dumped them in a pile on the foreshore.

The grass was shorter than it had been during the summer, and a mournful bleat from the hill behind told me why. Sam plonked himself down beside me and reached over to open the picnic basket. I slapped his wrist. "Hands off, sunshine. You boys have a job to do before you get fed."

We left the food where it was and made our way up the hillside towards the tumbledown building set against the cliff. Far across the field to our right the ruined buildings slumbered on, continuing their slow process of dissolution, and the yellowing leaves of the sycamores shook slightly in the gentle breeze. The sea was almost dead flat, hardly a ripple disturbed the bay, and up on the hillside the sheep grazed undisturbed.

The landscape seemed calm and completely self-contained. It was hard to imagine that blood-shed and violence had ever been done in such a peaceful place. We entered the ruined building, and crowded together in a patch of sunlight which had made its way in through the tumbled stones of the doorway.

Niall put his hand in his pocket and pulled out a red silk handkerchief. He shook it open and Sam caught a small plastic cylinder, which he held cupped in one hand. Niall unscrewed the top and carefully pulled out a rolled scrap of creamy paper. He opened the scroll and held it up to the light. The low afternoon sun gently illuminated the fragment, and I could see markings. On the reverse, a neat, anatomically correct drawing of a hand, bones and all, with the warm sunlight glowing through it. On the upper surface of the parchment, the effect of the sunlight causing it to appear as if the letters were superimposed upon the hand, a tall, curving *I*. A smaller *w*, crisply drawn. Other letters, in a mediaeval looking cursive script: a verse familiar to us all. *In the Beginning was the Word.*

Niall carefully rolled the paper and slid it back into the cylinder, closing it securely and wrapping it in the cloth again. He looked at Sam, and Sam nodded. Niall stooped slightly and entered the enclosure built around the great standing stone. Sam and I followed, squeezing into the tiny space.

Gently Niall knelt and pushed his little parcel into the recess set into the back wall. His fingers crept into the space, further back until his arm was almost at full stretch. He paused for a moment, and then he relaxed and withdrew his arm. His hand was empty. We made our way carefully back into the light, which seemed all the brighter by contrast with the small, dim place we had been sharing.

Niall stood for a moment, looking out over the scene. Then he stretched his arms out over his head, and bringing them down caught Sam in one and me in the other. He hugged us both for a moment, as the bright afternoon sunshine bathed the landscape in warmth, then set off across the field towards the picnic. I stood for a moment with Sam. He put his arm round my shoulders and rested his chin on my head, reminding me again that he'd grown during the summer. I breathed in the smell of him and hugged him back.

"Are you happy?" I asked.

"Oh yes, Mum, it's great. Are you okay with it?"

"I like Niall," I said. "I always have. Of course, it was a bit of a surprise, but if you're happy, then I'm happy. But there's one thing I don't understand."

"Hmm?"

"What about Annette?"

Sam pulled away slightly and looked at me. "What about her?"

"Well, you told me she used to be Niall's girlfriend. So I naturally assumed he preferred girls. But here you are, together. Does he play both sides?"

I had to stop. Sam snorted with laughter and bent over holding his sides, giggling. "Oh, Mum, I love you."

"What? Is he bi or something?"

"Stop it, Mum. It hurts."

I pulled away from Sam and pushed my hands into my pockets. I didn't know what was going through his head, but clearly I'd been really dim. So dim that I still didn't understand what was so funny. Sam sobered and straightened up. He looked at me with a serious expression, although his face quirked with humour once more before he began speaking.

"I told you Annette used to be Niall's partner. I didn't tell you she used to be his girlfriend."

I looked at him blankly. Sam sighed and tried again. "Niall and Annette were at school together. Annette was his first love. Back then her name was Andrew. Niall stood by her all the way through the process of becoming a woman, full gender reassignment. But he says it didn't feel right to him, afterwards. They still work well together. They're friends. You've seen them; the physical relationship is over, but sparks still fly. I've had to accept that she'll always be a part of his life, but Annette had to let him go. I think she'll always find that difficult."

I stared at him. Slowly what he had told me began to make sense. I had one more objection.

"But she's so beautiful."

"Yes, she is. I think she always was. It must have been hell growing up like that, always knowing you weren't what you appeared to be. I know she's prickly sometimes, but I really like her. Most of the time."

"My wonderful, caring, loving son. I must have done

something really good in a past life to have been given you."

"Shut up." Sam was embarrassed. Then he relaxed his body into mine again and hugged me, my head to his chest. I could feel the vibration of him giggling again.

"What?" I demanded, pulling back to look into his face.

"Best not to tell Dad," he said with a wicked grin.

In my mind's eye I looked over that glorious, cream-skinned, red-headed voluptuous creature.

"Andrew," I said. Sam sniggered.

"You're right. We definitely won't tell Dad."

THE END

16398504R00110

Printed in Poland
by Amazon Fulfillment
Poland Sp. z o.o., Wrocław